SOMEWHERE

IN THE

To Meredith
With sincere gratitude
Enjoy Reading

SHADOW

Asib Coulibaly

Louisville Oct 29, 22

SOMEWHERE

IN THE

SHADOW

ABIB COULIBALY

atmosphere press

To my wife and kids
for all their love and support.

To the memories of Baidy Ba,
who succumbed to gun violence in Milwaukee.

And to my friend Souleymane Sakho,
who untimely passed away.

PART

ONE

CHAPTER
ONE

Amar awoke abruptly, shaken by his own laughter. He remained in a state of semi-consciousness, his mind wading between the real and the unreal until his body recovered mechanically, almost heroically. Through the diffuse light, he could not distinguish anything that resembled a field of corn or mangoes as in his dream... He was in a bed... far from the time and place where his dream had occurred. He stood still for a moment, wanting to make the most of this moment of innocence. It was so rare to find those precious moments.

It was still one of his childhood dreams where he used to spend a lot of time in the mango plantations to appease his hunger. It was often the same dreams he had, in the company of his young cousins frolicking carelessly through the sunlit mazes of the childhood realm.

Fatigue, aches and pains, long-time mischievous companions, quickly brought him back to reality with long pinches throughout his body. He looked through the dark room, listened to the monotonous sound of the central heating, with a forgotten smile on his lips. He did not have to meditate long because the alarm of the mobile phone suddenly went off, killing the remnants of drowsiness that lingered in his mind. He leaped out of bed and walked to the toilet. He only had about thirty minutes to clean up, do his morning prayer, swallow his coffee and rush to the bus stop...

He was frantically working to keep up the pace. The waiters stacked the dirty dishes, creating a huge mess on the narrow counter. Only the new busser was willing to do things right, at least for his first day of work, and took his time to sort out the different dishes and place them in the right order: the big plates for dinner, the medium for lunch, the small ones for salads, the colorful for dessert, the soup bowls, the pasta bowls... Mr. Frank, the owner of Frank Grill, often yelled at them to arrange everything and make it easier for the dishwasher, but as soon as he left, 'dish land' would turn into traffic without order or enforcement. Dishes were scattered everywhere, making his task even more difficult.

Bussers emptied half-empty glasses of water and placed them into racks. The glasses of champagne and beers were more carefully stored because they were more fragile and expensive. They emptied water or coffee in the sink, and sometimes, one of them by clumsiness or haste splashed him in the face. Amar never complained. What would be the point? He already knew that after the apologies, the same thing would happen again. The water, coffee and other beverage rack were placed on the top counter, preventing him and the servers from seeing one another. So, accidents always happened. He splashed people all the time, too, because he had to spray the dishes first, scratch off the fat and dirt before placing them into the machine. It was only when he heard someone complain that he realized what had happened. He would also mumble an apology and continue his work.

But he never did it on purpose, unlike his co-worker Abdu, who, when he was tired and angry, would spray blindly at the dishes, spraying whoever happened to be on the other side. Not only would he not apologize, but he would also argue when that person complained. Abdu had been in the US for so long, and for some reason, had developed a defiant and hostile attitude toward people. He was stubborn and never admitted he was wrong. He spared the owner and the manager for the only reason they were quick to fire people. Amar liked to work on the same shift with Abdu because they came from the same country and spoke the same language. They always found time to chatter about the latest news of the country.

Because Amar could hardly see people's faces, all he could see were hands hurriedly placing dishes on the counters and scampering like busy bunnies. The only hands he recognized were those of young David, who was the only black among the waiters and bussers. For the others, all he could tell from their hands was whether they were men or women. Pots, bowls, ladles, and greasy roasting pans were brought from the kitchen. He hated the roasting pans. They were huge, and he would waste so much time scraping the oily and greasy messes. Sometimes a huge jam was created by the kitchen staff and the servers bringing up dirty dishes and picking up clean ones.

In the peak of busy days, 'dish land' became the land of chaos, literally. The space was small and littered with mess while everybody was speeding to get their stuff ready. They wanted to satisfy the angry, starving, or impatient customers. It was Friday, the beginning of the weekend, and couples, families and friends would meet at the restaurant located in a small town west of Detroit. The population was overwhelmingly white, but it was only in these small towns that it was easy to find a job, especially a dishwasher job, because Detroit was a poor city with a high unemployment rate.

Employers loved to have African workers because they stayed in their jobs longer and were more flexible. They would endure all the dirty tasks that others balked at without protesting. They never asked for pay rises or took a vacation. They never called off sick for fear of losing their jobs. Employers would rub their hands together with such workers because, as they say, *'If you do not know your rights, you do not have any'*. Amar felt that America was the land of contradiction. Theoretically, everybody was born equal and had the same rights, but in practice, everybody was not treated the same. He thought the few educated Africans should help the uneducated majority to know more about their rights during the community meetings. But those people could not care less. All that mattered to them was to be able to put their hands on the meager paychecks of a few hundred dollars a week. And because they come from impoverished countries, that money means the world to them.

That small check in their hands can feed and take care of a whole family. That small check can be useful to a whole community based on solidarity and help. Thus, for them, missing a day of work was to take food away from a family, to deprive a patient of care, to prevent an important event from happening. As long as they had enough strength left to get to work, they would be there... often at the cost of their own health. Their own well-being did not matter. They were proud to protect and feed the extended family. And that pride transcends personal well-being.

Amar placed the plates on the racks and pushed them through the dishwashing machine. Twenty seconds later, he picked them up, sorted them and put them on the shelves. But also, he had to carry as many plates as possible in the kitchen to allow the servers or bussers to drop off more dirty plates. He had to place about twenty plates in each flat rack, push them successively in the machine and hurry to retrieve them from the other side, pick them up and put them away. Then, he would take them to the kitchen and start again. In the meantime, the silverware had to be taken care of as they were also needed anytime.

Sometimes a voice would yell from the kitchen:

"Dinner plates!"

And he had to hurry to carry them. Suddenly one hand pushed away from one of the water racks that was hanging on the top counter, and two blue eyes stared at him. "Are you hungry?"

He nodded. Of course he was hungry! He had been working for almost six hours without any break. John, the assistant manager, handed him a plate of grilled salmon served with brown rice. It was his lucky day because he liked grilled salmon. Probably an order mistake or a disgruntled customer who found out the salmon was not well cooked or blackened enough. It was an expensive meal, and the kitchen employees were not allowed to order it, but they were probably not going to throw it away. He was allowed to order a sandwich, some chicken, or a burger... nothing more. He tried to swallow his food as quickly as possible because he could not afford to stack too many dirty dishes for fear of facing the owner's raging voice. Chef Frank was always extremely nervous when the restaurant was very full or when it was terribly slow. Nature had not endowed him with the ability to manage extremes.

It was winter, and the restaurant was busy.

"Hey. You! Over there! Why you're doing that?" The dreaded voice of chef Frank roared, making the new pantry boy startle. He had been hired the day before and was responsible for baking the bread and filling the bread drawer.

"Listen! Never put fresh bread on top of the old one. You must flip them so the old bread can be used before it dries out. Do you understand?"

"Yes, Chef!" The poor soul replied in a small voice and went on quickly to flip the bread from the drawer. He had no idea that he had done the wrong thing. He was still being trained and had to learn most things the hard way.

A hand gently patted Amar in the back. He turned around and exchanged an expressive smile with the young blonde woman who had silently sneaked into the narrow space.

"How are you today?" She said in a soft voice.

"I'm fine, Christine. Yourself?"

"I feel wonderful." She said, beaming. She proceeded to grab some small plates and soup cups. She hesitated and came back to him.

"Hey, we might need silverware. It's getting busy out there."

"No problem. They will be ready in a minute."

"I will be right back for it, sir." She said in an alluring voice.

He loved the way she always approached him and whispered in his face. He took a deep breath to better inhale her discreet scent, which, for a short moment, eclipsed the strong smell of food. With a complacent smile, he sent a plate-filled flat rack through the dish machine while watching her briskly walking away. He was looking forward to this moment. He knew Christine's schedule by heart, and he was always delighted to see her. It gave him the strength to put up with the backbreaking job.

He loved her fascinating eyes. They were a mixture of landscape with a touch of blue sea, distilled in a green river, with small golden sparkles. An abundant and supple hair fell over her frail shoulders. She often tied it in a ponytail to release a welcoming and inquisitive face. Her complacent and easy-going manners attracted him when they first met in that same spot. Whereas everybody was trying to avoid the damp and dirty place and tiptoed their way to pick up a few plates or utensils and disappear hurriedly, Christine literally came to him and invaded his lonely little world.

He remembered the first day he was taken to the restaurant by Demba to apply for a dishwasher job. That was his second day in this country, and they had to drive from the Detroit black neighborhood to another city where almost everybody was white. He was so shocked by the swift change in population. The more they drove, the more he was getting nervous. He was almost shaking like a leaf when the manager told him he could start immediately, and Demba had to leave him all alone in the middle of all those white people. He struggled so much trying to understand their fast talking and feared that the slightest mistake would cost him dearly.

Failure and rejection were two of the reasons he traveled from his country to the US. As a child who lost his parents early, he had been raised by his uncle. He never felt accepted by his adoptive family, and as he grew, there seemed to be no place for him to thrive and be happy in his own country. He was not able to complete his studies at the University due to the lack of means and the high rate of student failure. After College, he was not able to secure a government job from the very selective and corrupt system. Companies were nonexistent, and nobody was hiring. He was a failure and was even denied love because of his low-class origin. He was rejected in his own country by people of his own skin color. How could he be accepted by people with different skin?

He was foreseeing all kinds of mean reactions and mistreatments from those people and was shocked when it turned out everything was different. People were kind and patient with him because of the language barrier. He felt even more accepted by his white co-workers than his black neighbors. America was such a strange place. He could not take that scene off his mind in the local grocery store when he tried to make that guy in front of him move forward because he was busy texting on his phone. He gently touched the guy on the shoulder to tell him the line was moving, and the man sprang like a tiger, yelling at him not to touch him again. He felt so embarrassed and uttered some quick apologies so the guy would not jump on him. That episode made him fear the black people, his black brothers. He could not help thinking that if a black man like him were about to punch him for touching his shoulder, maybe a white man would have stabbed or shot him. Yes! America was a strange place. A place of contrasts. The worst can happen when you expect the best. And the best can happen when you expect the worst. It helped him a lot when he had found out there was another co-worker, Abdu, who was from his own country. But Christine was truly the person that helped him feel relaxed and comfortable in his job.

She had asked him his name, insisted on pronouncing it right, and would come back whenever she could to lend a hand or just hang out with him during her break. He was a reserved man who liked to stay in his corner and take care of his work. By his rare moments of break, he would stand silently behind the washing machine and ruminate on the dark fate that had landed him into that narrow place. And sometimes Christine would come out of nowhere to bring a ray of sunshine into his dull life. He loved her vivacity, her joie de vivre and her free spirit. She liked to say funny things, and he struggled to detect the humor, but he was grateful for her attempts to extract a smile from him.

The first time Christine sneaked behind him to pick up plates, he had just thought it was another one of those impatient servers who could not wait and wanted to help themselves. He had not even taken the time to thank her. But she had come back whenever she could and got to work as if she were paid to help him. She would pick up the soup cups and silverware because that was part of her tasks, and then she would come back to help him with dinner plates and lunch plates, which was not part of her job. When he finally decided to thank her, ashamed of himself, she accepted with a simple nod of her head.

Christine had already vanished as quickly as she had arrived, but Amar was still smiling and thinking about her when Abdu interrupted his little daydream:

"When are you going to invite her?" He flinched and glanced at his co-worker who had just entered dish land. He was surprised by his question. How on earth was he able to get into the course of his thoughts? Had he suspected something between him and Christine? He was very wary of Abdu's mouth because he could be talkative and indiscreet, and that was what he needed the least at that moment. He pretended he did not understand.

"Who?"

"Who! The one who just came out of here with the most beautiful smiles. She only makes that kind of smile to you." Abdu grinned.

"You're just trying to tease me. Christine is a nice girl. It's just her nature." He tried to defend himself.

"Okay, buddy. You are trying to keep me in the dark. But remember. I am your 'bro'. And you'd better confess so I can give you some advice. Anyway, I am here in case you need somebody to talk to." He said with the air of someone who knew much more than he wanted to show.

"She's just a nice woman. We get along well, that's all." Amar said.

"You get along well with everyone. You are the nice guy here." Abdu said with a pinch of jealousy in his voice. "So that is not the problem. I see the way she looks at you, and I know what that look means," he added, winking at him and changing his tone.

Abdu was making him nervous. Did he know some-thing, or was it just a ruse to tease him and then read his reactions? Was it so obvious that he and Christine liked each other? It was true that no matter how filthy the place was, no matter how arduous the task was, when Christine showed up, everything became different for him. Her presence would turn the dim and sad room into an enchanted realm illuminated by a radiant smile and soft voice. Then, nothing could spoil the rest of his day. He smiled without realizing it. He was torn between the attempt to hide his joy of seeing Christine and his desire to keep a neutral face in front of Abdu, and that contrast gave his solemn face a curious expression. But the shine in his eye was too obvious, and he could not hide that. He was aware of it, and he wished his face were less expressive. It was not the time to let his guard down. If Abdu could so easily see his interest in Christine, then everyone else could too. He had to pull himself together because he did not want to lose his job over an affair. After all, Christine was just a co-worker. Dating a co-worker could be risky for everyone, even for normal citizens, let alone a stranger like him. Therefore, he had to be twice as careful. It was so easy for him to get in trouble and be deported because of his immigration status. A simple affair gone wrong could not only cost him his job, but also it could seal his fate and put him on the wrong side of the wall.

Not to make things any easier, the assistant manager, John, only had eyes for Christine, and that also could backfire on him. Christine was a beautiful and cool young woman. She could choose to go out with whoever she wanted, and thinking about the possibility that she might be interested in him made him feel important but also scared.

"And what do you think would have happened if I go out with her?" He could not help asking Abdu.

There was a bit of silence. At first, Abdu pretended not to hear; then he turned to Amar with an amused expression.

"What do you mean by, 'if I go out with her'?"

"I mean, we are good friends, but you know sometimes friendship can lead to something else." Abdu gave him an enigmatic look, and he felt he was going too far in his attempt for an explanation.

"Let me tell you something, my friend. There is no such thing as friendship between a man and a woman. Now, if I were you, I would not wait to ask her out. You know these women are just trying to have a little fun. They get tired of a relationship very quickly, and before you know it, they already turn their backs on you. You must 'beat the iron while it is still hot'."

In the time he had been working with Abdu, he had learned not to trust him because he had already displayed a sly personality on several occasions. So, the fact that he was hurriedly pushing him into Christine's arms raised some red flags in his head. Besides, what he was saying was not true about Christine. Rumors run sometimes in the restaurant about some women being players, but Christine's name had never been mentioned. She seemed to know what she wanted and mostly kept to herself and her job.

Amar did not want to be carried away into dreams and illusions, but sometimes reality makes it hard to resist. He was there to work hard and save money. Everything would have been simpler if Christine had given him the indifferent look that some co-workers did. If only she could just do her job without even taking the time to greet him or even glance at him! She was the only one who gave him that look that made him feel self-aware and visible; a look that got him out of his barricaded world and dug deep into his soul, stirring in him the debris of lost happiness.

One afternoon, Amar heard for the first time Christine being loud and talking furiously to the assistant manager. The latter must have had a beef against her and had allegedly thrown some mean words at her concerning an order mistake. She had turned into a tigress, and the whole kitchen was vibrating from her surprisingly vehement words. The assistant manager had to back down while the other servers tried to calm her. To his great surprise, Amar saw her rushing into dish land.

"Are you all right, Christine?" He timidly approached her.

"No" She yelled. She immediately rectified her tone, realizing she was no longer in the kitchen.

"Sorry, Amar. He drives me crazy!" She was still shaking with rage.

Amar had never seen her in such a state and was at a loss what to do. He hesitated for a moment, and then he rubbed her shoulders, trying to comfort her. "You'll be all right, Christine." He kept saying.

She suddenly looked at him and said: "You are such a nice guy." She took a deep breath and before leaving she said: "Can I hug you?"

He was caught off guard and simply nodded. They hugged as a shudder suddenly crossed both of their bodies, and she gently detached herself from him.

"See you later, Amar."

"See you, Christine."

Since that day, Amar felt that he was no longer the same, and something in him consumed his thoughts and put him in a state where he no longer wanted to be alone. Something that pushed him to do or say something, anything that would bring him closer to Christine. How did they get there? This question circulated obstinately in his mind, and he was not able to find an answer. He felt that, if he got closer to Christine, either out of love or friendship, he would discover a clue that would reveal to him the secret of the blistering fact that a person could walk past so many people every day and suddenly, when they meet somebody special to them, they feel like they never want to walk away again. That was how he felt when he looked at Christine...

He then reached a moment when he could not hold it anymore, and he asked Christine for a date. She had willingly accepted, to his greatest surprise. He had expected her to frown, to cast a horrible look at him, leave hurriedly and even denounce him in front of everyone. He had prepared himself to die of embarrassment. It was stronger than him, and he could not remember what he had mumbled to her at first. He had suddenly become a shy teenager again, stumbling over his words. His knees seemed to fail him, and droplets of sweat had formed on his forehead. At the very moment when he thought the sky was going to fall on him, she came to his rescue, took his hand, and leaned her adorable face towards him and, with a half-serious, half-amused voice, she asked him:

"Amar, are you all right? Do you need some water?"

He immediately felt guilty, avoided her unbearable blue gaze, and wanted to be somewhere else.

She had gently pressed his hands, shook him a bit as if

to pass on to him more energy, looked him in the eyes and said:

"Hey... Of course! I want to go on a date with you. However, you will have to repeat your request because I could hardly hear what you said." She had told him with an amused look.

"I want to know you a little more, and we could have... dinner somewhere." He managed to say.

"With pleasure, Amar." She had picked up a few dishes and stepped slowly backwards, smiling.

Of course, he could not reveal that to Abdu. He would find out in due time. For now, all he could think about was the date he was going to have with Christine in a couple of days... He left Abdu spray and wash while he went to the other end of the dish machine to retrieve the dishes and place them on the shelf. He was happy to finally have some help. Abdu came from his second job and was as tired as him. Abdu often chose to do the washing while he would take the clean dishes to the kitchen. Then, he would bring back all the dirty stuff from the kitchen for Abdu to clean. He was working faster than usual, filled with energy and excitement. "Two more days, and I will be the happiest man on earth." He kept saying to himself.

But somewhere in the back of his mind, he could not help thinking about the uncertain future a date with Christine could face. The ghost of the past came haunting him. He had already dated a girl in Africa and had learned the hard way that he could not date every girl. He was told her caste was superior to his, and they could not be a match. Christine was white and beautiful, but this is America, the land of the free and the land of opportunities, and that was why he loved that country so much.

CHAPTER
T W O

Amar got off the bus and was greeted by a gust of frigid wind that whipped him in the face. It was terribly cold, and he thought his coat was getting worn out, and he needed a warmer one. The weather was dreadful, and he was in danger of getting sick. The icy hell had taken over the universe, spreading its silver-like and dazzling lawn throughout the city. He thought of running to the apartment, but there was snow everywhere, and he did not want to fall on the slippery pavement. The fear of not being able to get up and getting buried under a shroud of snow made him hurry up to shelter as quickly as possible.

Like a hungry wolf, the wind howled and bit furiously on every segment of exposed skin. He adjusted his hat to better cover his ears; he had the feeling that an invisible force was viciously prickling them with a thousand sharp needles. He could barely feel his limbs and thought that only a tiny part of his brain was working, and the only thing he could think of was to reach the building at all costs, which was half a mile away.

Despite the cold, the streets were not empty. He passed through a small business center and saw homeless people in a remote corner. They were busy kindling a dying fire, which they fed with pieces of cardboard and other flammable materials. Other passers-by, wrapped in heavy coats, hats on their heads and scarves around their necks, were rushing to their destinations. The only sounds he could hear were car horns combined with the whistling of the wind. The snow, which had stopped for a short time, began to fall again. Small flakes fell, intensifying abruptly and making visibility almost impossible.

The snow was falling on and on and piled on the pavement, muffling the sound of footsteps. The noiseless movements of the pedestrians evoked the unreal scenes of a silent film, while the glow of an invisible sun gave to the daylight an anonymous face that could be dawn or evening twilight. Only the immense weariness that bent him almost in half and the hunger that cramped his stomach reminded him that it was an early evening, prematurely darkened by a sun knocked out by the onslaught of the snow.

He hurried down the sidewalk leading to the apartment building and shuffled painfully towards the entrance as if his whole life depended on it. He was greeted by the welcoming caress of the central heating. He took the elevator to the fifth floor and reached an apartment at the end of the hall. He took off his gloves and feverishly fished for his keys in his pockets. With a shaking hand, he opened the door, and after taking off his shoes, he rushed to the thermostat to see if he could turn up the room temperature. He found that it was already high. He quickly got rid of his coat and sank into the couch in the living room.

He was still shaking badly and spent the first minutes trying to feel his limbs struck in profound numbness. He rubbed his hands vigorously against each other to bring them back to life, trying several movements, folding and unfolding his legs, twisting his fingers and neck. Slowly, he felt his body coming back to life.

Gradually recovering his senses and mind, he listened for a human presence in the apartment and realized that he was alone. The others had not yet returned from work. He shared the apartment with Demba and Gora. It was a three-bedroom apartment, and he had lived there for a long time, but they were rarely present at the same time. Demba was a taxi driver, and Gora worked in an auto parts factory. He felt exhausted every night after coming home from work.

He went to the freezer and grabbed a bowl of Jollof rice. He took a plate, helped himself and put it in the microwave. He loved the spicy smell of stuffed fish as the tomato-sauced rice simmered in the micro. He was tired but happy. Tomorrow was the day of President-elect Obama's inauguration. He was looking forward to listening to the speech of the new president, the first black president of the United States. It was a historic moment, and he did not want to miss it. Fortunately, he had to work in the afternoon, and he would have time to watch the official ceremony on TV.

The following morning, Amar was the first to get to the apartment. He wished his roommates could be there on time to listen to the speech together. This was one of those big events even more exciting to them than the Super Bowl or the NBA final. This was about them, and they had all hoped together, dreamed together, and it would have been fabulous to cheer together and enjoy this moment of victory. The door of the apartment suddenly opened. Gora came in, followed by Demba. From the door, Gora was quick to inquire when he saw Amar, "Had it started yet?"

Amar immediately knew he was talking about Obama's speech.

"Not yet, but the inauguration ceremony has." He replied happily. They sank on the couch, their eyes glued to the TV screen. The speech had not yet begun, but the ceremony was underway with the presence of the distinguished guests, from both chambers, from the Supreme Court...

Obama carried on his frail back the immense hope of an entire forgotten community: the undocumented. He had talked about it a lot during the campaigns and promised that he would find a solution to it during the first hundred days of his reign. Amar himself was undocumented but compared to others who had spent more than a quarter of a century in this country and had left their spouses and children behind, he often forgot his case. For them, America did not represent this country of freedom symbolized by the Statue of Liberty. For them, America remained the same country as it was five centuries ago, when the African slaves walked into the 'door of no return', to never go back, with no hope of seeing their families again.

Amar thought of Kadim, one of their fellow citizens. He could not look at him without a broken heart. Arrived in this country at the age of thirty-five, he had spent twenty-eight years in this country, had not attended the last days of his two parents; one of his two wives and two of his children also died. Five close people were buried without him, not to mention other relatives and friends. He had not attended the weddings of his children or the birth of his grandchildren. And yet Kadim kept an unwavering faith in the future and congratulated all those he had met during Obama's victory because, he said, all their prayers and desires were heard by God: "The long-awaited moment had come. Soon the new president will legalize us, and we will all be able to visit our families. Amen!" He would solemnly say. Kadim had repeatedly considered returning home, but he had to give up because even at his age, he was still his family's main source of income.

Across the screen, the eyes of the entire black community of the country sparkled with hope and pride. Africans, especially undocumented immigrants, all felt the same way. "His father was from Kenya, and he had never forgotten his roots. He will not forget about our community. He will keep his promises." They said among themselves. At last, one of their own had been elected, and he was going to free them from this giant prison called America. At last, they would visit their close family, find loved ones, say goodbye to those who had left them.

Washington's place was packed with people, and the scene seemed unreal as all eyes were on the slender man and his black family, who had the huge responsibility of leading the greatest nation in the world. People wanted to capture every second of this precious moment as history was unfolding.

There was a dead silence in the room when President Obama started his speech:

"... The time has come to reaffirm our enduring spirit; to choose our better history; to carry forward that precious gift, that noble idea, passed on from generation to generation: the God-given promise that all are equal, we are all free, and all deserve a chance to pursue their full measure of happiness ..."

"... In reaffirming the greatness of our nation, we understand that greatness is never a given. It must be earned. Our journey has never been one of short-cuts or settling for less. It has not been the path for the faint-hearted – for those who prefer leisure over work, or seek only the pleasures of riches and fame. Rather, it has been the risk-takers, the doers, the makers of thing – some celebrated but more often men and women obscure in their labor, who have carried us up the long, rugged path towards prosperity and freedom..."

He was talking in general terms about the Americans, about the collapse of the economy, about terrorism gaining ground... and they all were listening to see if he was going to talk about the undocumented immigrants. He had not alluded to them, but there was hope. He had promised that he would take the situation of the undocumented into his own hands because most of them had left their country in the hope of having a better life, of helping those who had remained in the country and were facing hunger, disease and needed support for a decent living; and that was not against the American dream, on the contrary... And as the new President-Elect had said it well: "... and all have the right to pursue the full measure of happiness."

They had all come to seek happiness and worked hard for it. Amar told himself that he spoke well and that he thought well of them, and at some point, as he had promised, he was going to grant them work permits, give them permission to visit their families and friends. That was all they wanted. For the most part, they did not even need the coveted US citizenship. Above all, they wanted to be a citizen of the world. A world where happiness is possible when you work hard. They work a lot harder than most people. All they want is the right to happiness, the freedom of movement...

Most of Amar's fellow citizens had left their country with only the teachings of their venerable spiritual guide, whose messages resonated more current than ever in the contemporary world. "Work as if you were never going to die, and worship God as if you were going to die tomorrow."

"I am a little disappointed. I did not hear him specifically talk about us." Demba said at the end of the speech.

"But we should admit he made a beautiful speech," Amar said.

"A beautiful speech? What do we need a nice speech for? I am talking about a solution for the immigrants. He did say he was going to find a solution in the first hundred days." Gora growled. He was visibly not happy.

"You're so impatient that you don't listen to yourself talking," Demba said. "You said in the first hundred days. I remind you that today was his FIRST day."

"In our country, they say: 'Before a good meal can taste good, it has to smell good first'. And what I have heard in this speech doesn't 'smell that good'."

Knowing that it was futile to convince Gora, Amar turned to Demba, who was much more amenable.

"I believe he will take care of us. We have to be

patient."

"Obama is the best thing that could happen to us. We have to keep faith in him." Demba agreed.

"As far I am concerned, all that matters is a president who gives papers. We are tired of rotting in this country and not being able to visit our sick and old parents. No beautiful speech in the world can replace that." Gora gesticulated angrily.

He seemed to be addressing an invisible enemy, and his anger could backfire on anyone at any time. Amar and Demba simply nodded. Even though Gora spoke more often with the heart than with the head, he could not be blamed for telling the truth. There was a lot of compassion in the new president's speech, but concrete action for the undocumented would speak louder than any beautiful speech. Besides, neither of them wanted to upset Gora because he could be very impulsive and agitated, especially when it was a sensitive or personal matter. Demba did not have too much time as he had just come to change, pray, and eat before returning to his cab. On a normal day, he never spent more than thirty minutes in the apartment, except at night to sleep. Amar felt too tired to try to discuss with Gora. Like most of them, Gora had not seen his parents for more than a decade. That was eating him so bad. And sometimes he felt like he wanted to strangle somebody to let off some steam.

Gora could be violent, and the fact that he was heavily built was not helping. He would often pick a fight with people, and Amar had repeatedly feared for his life. Fortunately, he and Demba were calm in nature. But despite that, tragedy had almost struck one day. It was in the middle of a meal; Gora had become angry with Demba because he had made fun of him. They were 'joking cousins', which means some ethnic groups are entitled to make fun of each other. Demba was Pular and Gora was Serer. Pular and Serer can poke fun at one another anytime because of some ancestral pact, and none of them should take it badly. But that day, Gora was in one of his bad moods, and he had not taken the joke well. He did not want to attack Demba in front of Amar, because he did not want him to intervene; he had simply followed Demba into his room and locked the door behind him. He was much stronger than the frail man and had thrown himself upon him like an enraged lion. Amar had rushed to the door and knocked in vain. It all happened so fast. He heard Gora yelling, "Repeat what you said, and you will regret it!"

Amar could barely hear Demba's choking voice through the door. Something told him that Gora was strangling him. He knew he had to act fast before the irreparable happened.

"Listen to me, Gora!" He screamed through the locked door. "If you don't open that door in this very second, I'll call the police. Do something stupid and you are never going to see your parents again. How can you act like this, Gora! Open this door. Right now!"

He then prayed that it would not have to come to that. Calling the police was risky for all three of them. That could lead to their deportation. As if by a miracle, the door had opened. Gora seemed to have recovered his mind after roughing up Demba for a few minutes. He walked past Amar without looking at him, shirtless and sweaty. Amar stood in front of the door, unable to take a step forward as Demba coughed violently and sobbed like a little boy on his bed. He had just suffered the humiliation of his life. He was in his late fifties, had left wives and children back in the country, and now he had just been bullied by a man much younger than him. He had gone through all the hardships of life; thought he had seen them all and most time laughed them off because hardships are parts of the foundation that strengthen a man's character. But being brutalized that way for a futile joke was more than he could take.

In Africa, Gora would have paid for his act dearly because Demba's children would never have accepted that. Here he could not even go to the police because he was already considered an outlaw. He was already living like a person on parole, and like any person in a position of weakness, anyone could abuse him without him being able to speak up or denounce them. America had become a vast prison for him and for many others. Eleven million prisoners. Eleven million people were convicted just for pursuing their dreams. The same dream that, some centuries ago, was pursued by those who had built this country in the name of freedom.

Amar had returned to his room, and for three days the three roommates had avoided one another. Gora finally realized his blunder and wanted to apologize to Demba in front of Amar. Demba and Amar had kept that incident in mind and took it into account when they talked to Gora because he got carried away too easily even though he had a very generous heart. He earned a little more money than them, and he always wanted to spend more on bills and rent. His biggest flaw was his bellicose attitude. He had lost many opportunities because of his bad temper. But his colleagues at the auto factory seemed to understand him, and everyone respected him for his hard work, his cheerfulness when he is in a good mood and of course, his imposing physique.

Amar was proud to have witnessed a black president in the United States. It was the culmination of more than four hundred years of struggles, and the tears of the Reverend Jesse Jackson told a lot. Obama had flaunted his class, his intelligence, his open-mindedness. But above all, he had come to this position thanks to his education. Amar suddenly remembered with an aching heart that he was once called an educated man and realized how his life had turned from a young student full of dreams to an undocumented immigrant, forced to do some low-level entry job to survive. He had paid for his naivety and negligence. He wanted to read to relieve himself. He rummaged through his luggage and grabbed one of his old books he used to read in search of knowledge. Now he was just reading so he could sleep.

CHAPTER
THREE

The place was crowded with many Asians but also people from different backgrounds and countries. It was a buffet located near a movie theater on West 12 Miles, and not far from Telegraph Road. After watching a movie, they headed to the Vietnamese Buffet. As soon as they were sat, Christine headed for the seafood, whereas Amar, who was not a big fan, turned to the meat dishes. Pork, chicken, beef, grilled or sautéed, pasta, rice, beans, fries, or Vietnamese specialties were nicely displayed on the counters and frequently filled by alert cooks. Both were starving and went directly for entrees, ignoring the salads and soups.

While enjoying his grilled beef, Amar thought about how good it felt to be on the bright side of life for once, and not suffocating in his little space in dish land. So far, life for him was limited to his work and his apartment. He sighed silently and was already grateful to Christine. He had never thought, even in his wildest dreams, of finding himself in such pleasant company: a white, young, and beautiful woman. Christine obviously seemed happy to be there. She seemed to enjoy every moment of the ceaseless movement of people walking between the tables and the self-service buffet.

"I like the diversity of this place. Different people, different food. It is like an international seminar. Quite the opposite of our restaurant, where we usually have the same old white folks." Christine said.

"I absolutely agree with you. I assumed it would change you a little bit from the kind of restaurants you are used to." Amar replied.

"Don't assume anything. I have had African American friends and have been invited to places you might not even suspect."

"Really?" He said, a little surprised. "And what might be those places?"

"It could be anywhere from restaurants to parties..." Christine said in an enigmatic voice.

"Hum!" Amar nodded, his nose dipping into his plate. "I hope you like it here."

"I love it!" Christine exclaimed.

He wondered how the restaurant could make money with all those customers making several trips to refill their plates. There were some customers that were especially hunting for seafood. Crabs, oysters, and shrimps would disappear as soon as they were brought. It was 'all you can eat', and that kind of business would never have flourished in his country back in Africa. There were so many famished people that they would just spend the whole day eating inside the restaurant.

"Tell me about yourself," the soft voice of Christine pulled him out of his thoughts,

"I am from Africa. But you already know that... My parents died in a car accident when I was very young, and my paternal uncle took me with him. He had two wives who took turns abusing me because they were too frustrated with their own lives and too busy with their own children. So, I lived and grew up in a difficult environment, often beaten and deprived of food and..." He paused. "Why am I annoying such a beautiful woman with my sad life?"

"Because the 'beautiful woman' wants to hear about your 'sad' life." She said while struggling to extract the flesh from a crab leg.

Amar could not understand how so much effort could be made for such little food. With chicken or beef, that would never have been an issue. There would be plenty of meat to bite instead of rummaging food through some horrible creature bones. He thought she was being sarcastic, but something in the tone of her voice told him that sadness was not something new to her. He knew that some dark memories had just crossed her mind from the brisk and nervous manner she broke the crab's leg. He wanted to pull his own hair for bringing her to this place and find nothing to tell her other than his sad past. He tried to find in his head a funny thing to say, but he could not get rid of the uneasiness that filled him for starting a bad conversation, and he remained lost and confused for a moment, staring at the window where small snowflakes, flying in the wind, landed quietly on the grey windows.

"Do you know that I saw snow for the first time in this country?" He finally broke the silence.

"Your country must be beautiful. A country without snow is a heaven. If only I could live in such a country where the summer lasts forever..."

"It is hot ten months out of twelve in my homeland, and I must admit it is incredibly beautiful."

"So, what are you doing in this freaking country? Give me just one good reason." She said with amused eyes.

"It is more complicated than you think. The beauty of the landscape and the clemency of nature do not always make the quality of a country. Nature is ruthless in this side of the world, but men are taking care of things by building and repairing. In my country, nature is lenient and benevolent, and we do not take any advantage of it. On the contrary, we squander our natural resources. And the contrast is obvious: if you work hard here you can have a decent life. In Africa, even with hard work, you can barely survive." The specter of another sad reason why he traveled to America crossed his mind. America is truly the country of the free. He had loved a girl once but was denied the right to date her just because his ethnicity or caste was deemed inferior to hers. But that he could not reveal to Christine.

"I find it hard to follow you. But I admit that the few images and movies I saw on Africa are not very... flattering." Christine said, pulling him out of his thoughts.

"Unfortunately, what you saw is only the tip of the iceberg. The issues are even more serious with bad governance, political instability, the spoiling of natural resources... But to get back to the snow. I will never forget my first snow. I had no idea it would snow that day, and I did not have a coat on, only a jacket on my way to the bus stop. I did not understand why everybody else was wearing coats. Minutes later, a frigid wind suddenly began to blow, and I started to see some strange small white particles flying in the air. Then, big flurries were all over me as my jacket had no hood. I saw people covering their heads, and I understood my mistake. I was starting to shake so bad, and I didn't wait for the bus. I renounced my trip to the store and just sprinted back to the apartment. Once at home, shivering and terrified, I realized that I had just experienced the first snow of my life. The lesson I learned from that was you should never venture out in winter without checking the weather forecast."

"Yeah, the snow can be very mean if you are not well prepared." She admitted.

"By the way, tell me about yourself." Amar was eager to know more about her.

"My life is not as cheerful as you must have thought. And I do not want to add more sad things than what you have told me about you. It is better to talk about other things because we are here to have fun, aren't we?" A sparkle of joy lit in her blue eyes, adding more warmth to the coziness of the place.

"You're right. It is snowing and I hate the snow. But because you are here with me. I want it to snow so hard until *time* itself gets frozen and eternity, with its mighty wings, set up a tent in heaven where I could admire your beauty forever." He said, gesturing with his hands.

"Wow! I did not know you had a talent for poetry. It is beautiful and very flattering." She exclaimed, and then added with a sigh. "If only there were a way to escape reality, just time to get your head around things..."

"I do not think running away from reality is a solution or a good choice. It is that same reality that we are trying to shun that brings us together and leads to our meeting. You are here in front of me, and you are very real. Reality can be harsh, but it can be a source of inspiration and happiness. Illusion and dream can barely bring happiness." Amar said in a solemn voice.

She considered him, surprised.

"That sounds deep. Without dreams, reality can be unbearable, though."

"I know... And it is finding a balance between reality and dream that we can find ourselves and hope to have a meaningful life."

She meditated a moment about what he said.

"I was the unique child, and I was rather spoiled. But as I grew older, life became more complicated. My parents' marriage was falling apart, and as a teenager I had to witness them tearing each other apart."

"Then I left home very young to move in with my first sweetheart. He was adorable, and we were living life to the fullest, with the recklessness of the young mind. He was goodhearted, kind, funny, handsome... everything I wanted, but he had one weakness: drugs. He dragged me into his world, and I became addicted. It got worse and worse until we both overdosed... He did not make it. That was the end of the happy chapter in my life."

Amar could see the emotion resurfacing in her glistening eyes, and he reached out and put one hand on hers:

"I am so sorry to hear that... You don't have to..."

"I will be fine. She said with a faint smile. It feels good to talk to somebody who can understand you... Then I met Mark, my son's father, who reminded me of my own father. He was mean and possessive and made me realize that good men are an exception in this life. We would fight every day, and it got worse when he realized I was pregnant. He did not want a child, and I did not want to get rid of it. He chose to leave me, so I had to take care of myself and my baby." She gulped a glass of water as it could help her sink all the sorrow linked to that period of her life.

"Life can be cruel, but you are a brave young lady." Amar could feel her pain and her loneliness. He squeezed her hands.

They let themselves be lulled by the magic of the moment. Without knowing each other too much, they both had enough confidence in each other to address so easily the painful moments of their lives. Those sensitive periods of life that are delicately hidden from exposure during first encounters. It was as if they mutually wanted to take an emotional refuge into each other and unload every bitterness and sadness, which in return, was transformed into positive and vibrant energy by the power of a caring and welcoming heart. Listening to the sorrow of a soul of another always dampens one's own. They felt connected and were grateful to each other.

Returning from the date, Amar lay on his bed, staring dreamily and thoughtfully at the ceiling. He had had a wonderful date, and he could not stop thinking about her. When he went to sleep, he dreamed of her. They played hide-and-seek through the fields of his childhood, and the young woman's hair floated in the wind, blending into the blond tassels of corn rows. He chased her to the top of the hills, and both, breathless and radiant, received the last caresses of the setting sun. He woke up with his arms clenched around the pillow and realized how hollow existence could be without the promises of love...

CHAPTER
FOUR

At the wheel of his taxi, Demba was speeding along the 8 Mile Road. Traffic was quite fluid at this time of the day. He knew that route very well. It was at the limit of the cities of Detroit, Southfield, Farmington Hill and Livonia. Driving in these quiet little towns changed him from the busy and tumultuous streets of downtown Detroit, where finding a place to park was a feat. Some of his customers who worked in downtown Detroit and lived in the suburbs would take the bus after work to the city limits of Detroit and take a taxi for the rest of the ride home. It was more convenient for them than driving through the busy downtown Detroit. Thus, in the early morning and late afternoon, he would commute to take those customers in pools of two or three in his grey deadbeat van. Between rush hours, he would devote himself to African customers, especially women who worked in hair salons.

The hair salons opened a little later in the morning, and most of the African hair stylists were not driving. His days were very busy between Thursday and Saturday, as African hair salons were scattered throughout the city of Detroit, between the West Side and the East Side that divided the city into two parts. He liked to drive along 8 Mile Road, which allowed him to get from one side of the city to the other without wasting too much time. For now, he was just dropping off Fatima. She worked in a salon at 7 Mile Road on the West Side. It was an easy ride for Demba as it was not far, and the agreed minimum fare between the braiders and African drivers was ten dollars. Most African Hair salons littered along the 7th and 6 Miles on both the West Side and the East Side. He mostly avoided the 6 Mile and the 7 Mile, known for the indiscipline of their motorists. So, he stayed as long as possible on the 8 Miles before veering on the ultimate junction to drop off his customers. He knew all the salons' names and their owners and their employees. He knew those who were punctual, those who were never ready on time and made him wait, the impolite, the stingy, the capricious ones. So, when he got busy, he always prioritized the generous and the polite customers and only took the others when he had no more priorities.

Fatima was one of his favorite clients because she was respectful and polite. Most of these braiders earned much more money than their husbands and ended up looking down at them. They often came from homes where the man was used to being the breadwinner. As their purchasing power increased, and some of them supported entire families, including men, they took more and more the men's role and became less and less submissive. That situation usually brought conflicts between them and their husbands and was the cause of several divorces.

Many men had regretted bringing their wives because once they arrived and realized that their husbands were not the rich and powerful men who had often made them dream, once they discovered that their husbands lived only off odd jobs and that they did not belong to the middle or rich class in America, they started to treat their men with less respect. And because the law is more likely to be on their side, some women took that opportunity to make life even harder for their husbands.

Men who lived in these difficult situations often had only one choice, divorcing their once docile and caring wives, who had become dismissive and careless. Some men resorted to violence, but it would quickly turn against them because, in this country, women had the same rights as men, or perhaps more, unlike in Africa, where one could abuse one's wife and children without being worried.

For some women, it was a whole different story. They happened to marry complete strangers, and once they came to the States, they discovered the true color of their husband. Fatima belonged to that category. She was married by her parents to a distant cousin who lived in the US and saw a beautiful picture of her. After he had seen Fatima's picture while he was visiting another cousin in Detroit, Seku had made a connection with Fatima's family and started sending presents and money. He told them he was looking for a wife. What sensible girl did not dream of a charming prince living in the big city that came to pull them out of the hard chore and the poverty of small villages? What parents did not dream of a rich son-in-law that would send money and presents from the rich white country? The young and beautiful Fatima was married and taken to the US by Seku, thinking that the doors of paradise were opening for her. She dreamed of coming to the US and renovating her poor parents' shabby hut into a beautiful brick-made house, where they would not have to worry about being wet in the middle of the night in the rainy season. But all her dreams crumbled when she set foot in America. Seku was not the soft-spoken and generous man on the phone. It took him only a week to show his true face...

Fatima did everything she could to not let her misery appear and hid the traces of abuse she was suffering from her husband. The alcohol-mined man could not hold a job for three weeks and poured his anger on his wife, whom he would abuse every night when she returned tired after a long day at work. Fatima had to take care of her husband and children. Seku had ended up as a stay-at-home dad with the children during the day, and at the end of the day, he would snatch the hard-earned money of his wife, call her names for returning home late, and he would go out at night only to come back in the early morning, after getting drunk and having his pockets emptied.

Demba knew the story of all the braiders from their own gossiping. All he had to do was listen as they gossiped at each other when they were taking a ride. Their stories and private lives would be told in turn in the taxi, where he sometimes became a counselor for those who felt the need to confide because he was looked upon as a wise man who kept only to himself. They trusted him because he would never take advantage of the loneliness and sorrow of these young women, even though he was living in solitude for so long and was himself in deep need of care and attention.

Demba was particularly sorry for Fatima because he

was aware of all her troubles. She had remained brave in her ordeal, and it was hard to detect in her beautiful face a touch of sadness. She forced herself to look elegant, polite, and respectful, and Demba thought that among all his clients, she was the one who least deserved to have a brutal husband. Life seemed so unfair to that good lady.

On many occasions, Demba had scratched his throat to start a serious discussion with her but had always refrained at the last moment. He feared being told that it was none of his business. Unlike the others, Fatima was always silent and thoughtful. She just exchanged a few polite words and kept quiet the rest of the ride. She had no idea that Demba had heard of her troubles with her husband. She had received an upbringing where she had to bear every whim from her husband. It was said husbands hold the key to paradise for their wives. She also agreed to suffer for her children because, according to popular belief, if she wanted her children to be successful in the future, she would have to endure suffering and humiliation. The more she endured, the more they became successful in the future.

Fatima, however, began to have her doubts about those beliefs because as her children grew up, she felt that they were secretly developing some hatred for their abusive father. Jalika, her eldest daughter, had many times asked her with tearful eyes why their dad behaved that way:

"I hate him, mommy. He had no right to treat you like that. You should call 911 on him." She told her one day.

Fatima looked at her daughter with a horrified look:

"How can you say that about your own dad!" She yelled at her angrily.

"He is not my dad. He is just a monster," the girl whimpered.

The slap went off and landed on Jalika's cheek as she let out a scream of surprise. She sprang up and looked at her mom, confused and lost as if she were looking at a different person.

"Why do you hit me, mom?" Tears were streaming down her face as she tried to rush out of the room, but Fatima caught her and dragged her toward herself.

"I am so sorry, my love. I didn't mean to... You just scared me when you talked like that. Jalika, you are my heart. Promise me! You have always been a good daughter. Promise me you will stay a good daughter to me... and to your father".

"But why he is being mean to you and us..." she sobbed.

"He is just going through some hard times, but he loves us all. He used to be a good man. He is not like that." She patted her daughter and hugged her, trying to convince herself that she was right. She felt ashamed about her gesture towards her daughter, and to the fact that she had to lie to her children that their father was a good man. She thought she would never raise a finger against her children and just realized how violence was contagious. Seku was being violent to her, and now, that violence was spreading to her and her kids, and she could not even tell to what extent the damage had been done. All she knew was it had to stop before it was too late.

Jalika kept sobbing, and her siblings, who were playing in the living room, stormed into the master room. They never saw their sister so shaken, and they instantly joined and cried with her.

———

"Are you sure you're okay, Fatima?" Demba, who was watching her through the rear-view mirror, made a last attempt to start a conversation.

"I am fine, thank you." Demba's voice pulled her from her thoughts. Despite her family troubles, Fatima had no desire to talk about it. The only moments she talked about it were when she hid in her room, in her husband's absence, to talk on the phone with her mother who was back in Africa, too far away and too old to be of any help to her.

Demba rarely deviated from his rules of staying silent and letting customers initiate the conversation. But he had heard of Fatima's sad story and would have liked to give her advice. She was a lovely woman, still young and beautiful, but she was aging prematurely because of grief and suffering.

Fatima got out of the taxi with the youngest of her children, who was just two years old. Seku had refused to keep him at home because he cried a lot and prevented him from sleeping during the day.

The more he left the West Side and headed for the East Side, the difference became more apparent, and it was not surprising that the East Side was infested with gangs and criminals of all kinds because of unemployment and poverty. Between rides, Demba liked to park at a gas station located on Grand River Avenue. Grand River, or the M5 highway, separated the city of Detroit from that of Redford. The gas price in that gas station was always among the lowest in the city, but the place was also one of the most insecure. There were times of the night when it was dangerous to wander in the corner. During those times, gangs would take over the place to sell drugs and keep an eye out for potential rivals. This could escalate at any time, and the police were often on the lookout. The bus from Downtown Detroit had its last stop just behind the station, where some of Demba's customers would take a taxi to get home safely.

Not far away, just across the street overlooking one of the Grand River neighborhoods, three teens were hanging out, Mike, Tony, and Nick. They were all school dropouts, and Nick, the last one to be expelled, was telling them about the incident:

"That was so much fun. The science teacher was absent, and we had that old substitute that did not care much about us. She would bring a book and sit there and read. I was getting bored, so I grabbed the bag of that spoiled kid. You think there were books inside? Nope, only bags of chips, candies and cookies. I pulled them out and gave them away to the whole class. Everybody was cheering loudly, jumping and catching candies thrown in the air. The class was like a football pitch. I had never had so much fun. I am officially expelled." He victoriously raised his hand like he was holding a trophy.

"You did the right thing, bro," Mike said. "There is no need wasting your time in school, feeling like a prisoner between four walls and listening to stories that make you sleep, or trying to apply abstract rules in sciences, monitored by teachers, mostly white, who only cared about their paychecks. Those teachers did not care about black communities."

"I agree, brother. School does not correspond to our reality. We need to know how to be tough and how to survive the police, and school does not provide those subjects." Nick said, laughing.

"Talking about being tough, I have something to show you," Mike said.

"What is it, bro?" Tony asked. He was the most silent one because he stuttered a lot, especially when he was nervous.

Mike pulled out the object he had hidden in his jeans under the bemused gaze of his two companions.

"Dang! Man! Where you get this from!" Nick said, with his eyes shining.

"Shh... It is a secret I would not tell you. How I found one is not important. I told you I would find one."

What he did not want to tell them was that the gun belonged to his mother's boyfriend, and he did not want him to find out. He would beat him to death while his mother would watch helplessly. One day, he would make him pay every ounce of abuse. He was sharpening his plan, and once it was ready, that loser would see what he was capable of. He was going to make him pay for all the bad treatments he had done to him. For now, he was proud to show his peers that he was able to get a gun. It was an important step to be considered as a tough guy. He wanted to be a bad boy... and a terribly bad one. He had impressed his friends, and they were squeezing him with questions.

"Do you know how to use it? Have you ever used it? How many times? Hell, how did you do that?

"Yeah, it is crazy, we will have fun.

They talked and talked... while Mike felt more and more important and adopted the manner of someone who was used to handling this kind of object for a long time and pretended to know a lot more than he did.

"Of course, I know how to use it. If not, why would it be in my hands otherwise? We sure will have a good time. He said with a condescending grin that intrigued his friends. He felt like a superstar.

All three were fifteen years old. He was the youngest, the last to be fifteen, but the first to possess a gun.

"Dude, you really look mean," Nick said excitedly while bumping his chest against his like they were on a football pitch.

"That is so dope!" Tony said. They were so excited. They wanted to know what it felt like to use a real gun. They had played enough video games, and they needed to upgrade.

Mrs. Williams was quietly eating while considering her son, who was rushing to swallow his meal to return to the street. She had always lived alone with her son, whose father was killed by gang members. She had fought and had always worked two jobs so that her son would not need anything. Nick had never run out of toys, clothes, and food. All her life, she had fought to preserve her son on the right path. She had brought him with her to church every Sunday, making sure he did his homework every night before going to bed. She had done everything possible to ensure that the young boy did not feel the absence of his father. Despite all her years of sacrifice, coaching and advice, Nick had ended up in the street. What hurt her the most was the fact that her son was so smart and that he had made her proud in elementary school by being an excellent student, earning a lot of awards and making her dream of a bright future for him. At the crucial moment when he had to take his destiny into his own hands, he had deliberately chosen the street, turning his back on a whole series of opportunities that would have given him access to successful careers and a full and happy life. She shook her head sadly and asked her son, who was about to leave:

"And now, what are you going to do with your life now that you have messed up your studies?"

"Don't worry, mommy. Everything will be fine, I promise." He said nonchalantly.

"How can everything be fine if you have not even finished high school, Nick? How can everything go well, tell me?" She was trying not to let her anger explode, but she was visibly exasperated.

"Don't go there again, Mom. You know that putting yourself in such a state is not good for your high blood pressure. I am old enough to know what I want to do with my life. School, diplomas, all this is nice, but it is useless. I have no desire to end up like you, trapped between two jobs, just to pay the bills and never enjoy life."

"That is how I fed you, Nick. I did everything a mother had to do for her son, for you to succeed, to have higher degrees and a great career. What do you hope to achieve from the street? Tell me?"

She dared not go to the bottom of her thoughts for fear of resurrecting an old discussion they had had about Nick's father. Unfortunately, the boy was following the footsteps of the latter.

"I have to go, Mom. But to make you happy, I plan to find a job and then we will see for the rest. I love you, Mom." He kissed her quickly on her cheek and rushed outside.

She knew she had to pay attention to her diabetes and blood pressure, in addition to asthma, but more than all these diseases combined, her son was killing her a little more every day. Her son had been her strength and the joy of her life. She had never been happier than the day she had taken this little piece of man in her hands. She had been certain that she had finally had her revenge on life, which had never been kind to her, along with a violent husband, a drug dealer, and a man killer.

She was convinced that her life would change for the better. She had stopped drinking and smoking, caring about her health so that the baby would be born in the best conditions. She had grown closer to God by beginning to attend church. She had been doing two jobs so she could buy a house and prepare for her baby to come. She had sacrificed her life and leisure time, devoting herself entirely to the well-being and education of her little Nick. Now she could only contemplate with nostalgia the joyful moments captured in pictures of her little one, when he was still sweet and innocent. She had loved the moments when she shared her bed with her smart and adorable little boy, when she would read him stories at night and answer his questions full of curiosity and innocence. Nick had become the epicenter of her world, and she had imagined that when he grew up, he would become a great, respectable, and educated young man. She anticipated the pride she would feel in having raised an accomplished young man. She had never imagined it otherwise, and now she regretted seeing him grow up and become the kind of man she would never want to have raised, the spitting image of his late father. She could see the same attitudes, the same reactions, and the same mean eyes.

She felt like the father's demons had reappeared in the son, and she was trying to capture in her head the crucial moment when her son had gone astray and what she could have done to prevent it. She tried hard, but she could not figure out when she had lost her son because that boy who stood in front of her was just the shadow of her Nick. Her son was a kind little boy, intelligent, and smiling who loved to listen to her and make her happy. She did not recognize this boy who did not care about anything anymore. Neither about her nor himself. All of a sudden, she felt fear for what the future held for her: grow old and die alone in this house that she had sacrificed herself to buy and start a family.

Most of the youngsters in the neighborhood are gang members and die young or languish in prison. She had hoped and fought hard so her son would be among the few elected who got away from bad choices and attended good colleges. On closer inspection, she did not know if she could have done more than she had done. She felt that she would get sick by thinking too hard and looking for the cause of this failure that seemed to affect most of the homes around her. She got up from her chair, desperate and infinitely sad. She cleaned her empty table, then she sat in the corner of her couch, her eyes glued to the TV, watching the sad news of the day.

CHAPTER
FIVE

Now Amar relished his happiness of loving and feeling loved in turn. He felt liberated from the cage of solitude where he had been locked up for so long. His work took him too much time, and he had not had a lot of opportunity to go to the meetings organized by his community. Besides, he was a little introverted and did not feel comfortable around people. The few encounters he had had with the women in his community had often ended abruptly. He had finally given up and taken refuge in a past that he contemplated with bitterness. That past had followed him everywhere and had prevented him from pursuing a normal life.

Her name was Aisha, and she had been haunting his sleep for a long time. He had tried to bury that episode of his life in a remote corner of his memory, but it often came back much more vividly and disturbing than ever. One hot summer morning, he was roaming aimlessly through the neighborhood when he noticed a young woman in front of one of the rarely well-built houses of the street. She was standing by the front door and was staring at him as he walked by. Her deep brown eyes collided into his fleeting glance, and he could feel the impact that shuddered his whole body. Her intent gaze seemed to have an infinitely mysterious effect on him. Like a laser scan, it made its way directly to his heart and kindled small sparks that produced fireworks in his head and blurred his spirits.

He knew the girl must be a visiting relative like a thousand young people and students did during the long summer vacation. People did not go on vacation just like they did in Europe or America. When you have hardly anything to pay for food and utility bills, you cannot even dream of going on vacation like western people do. You just go visit some relative for a couple of weeks or months, sometimes just because there is nowhere else to go or nothing else to do. No summer jobs. No summer vacations. Only visits to the relatives if you can afford the transportation fees and you have your parents' permission.

Sometimes the relatives were not even told in advance. They knew when a cab stopped in front of the house, and a bunch of luggage was being unloaded. Then you had to go help your surprise guest and sometimes pay for the cab fee. It was the host family's duty to find them a room to stay in and take good care of them, even if they must borrow money for that. It would be offensive to have the honor of receiving a guest and not take care of them.

Amar did not remember if he greeted her or if it was the shivering of his lips that echoed into a rambling noise, making him speed up his pace. Neither did he remember her saying something, but he felt he was pursued by her gaze, and he turned into the first corner just for the sake of disappearing before his whole body melted like butter in the hot summer sun. The first thing he did when he was out of sight was stop and try to catch his breath. He did not know why he felt so confused, so lost, and so sad at the same time. He had come across hundreds of women in his life, and most of the time he did not even see them. He had never been obsessed or worried with them. The reason why he suddenly felt all that commotion inside him because of 'her' will remain a mystery.

He felt like going back and checking if she was real or if she was just a mirage of the deserted street. He realized he was sweating, and he was thirsty. He went through his pocket and could not find any coin to buy water. He could stay days without a penny in his pocket, and at his age, he was still living at his uncle's house, sharing a tiny room with three of his cousins, not even being able to contribute for food or bills. He had nowhere else to go except roaming in the neighborhood or hanging out with friends, playing draughts, hoping for an interview from the numerous applications he sent to teach in private schools. He tried public school multiple times but did not pass the exam, which was very selective. He pursued his morning walk because, for him, that was the only way to chase away all the dark ideas that haunted him.

He went back the following morning, and she was there again. For some unexplainable reason, he could not walk past her and found himself advancing towards her as if a drone inside him directed his steps. He smiled at her and stretched out his hand. She hesitantly shook his hand and he held hers, smiling foolishly. They both remained speechless, unable to detach their gaze from each other.

Aisha! When she uttered her name, it sounded like the sky had sent a thousand robins singing joyfully above his head. Blue was his favorite color, and it seemed to him the universe had replaced the dusty red sand with a brand-new blue carpet. They did not talk a lot, but she kept smiling at him! On his way back home, his eyes kept blinking. The sun looked too bright as he was literally dazzled by her beauty. It turned out she came for the summer to visit her uncle. She was born and raised in a faraway village, and that was her first time in this part of the country. It was supposed to be the best summer! Even without a job or money, if he could just behold her a few minutes every day, he would be the happiest man on Earth.

By the third day, Amar asked Aisha to take her for a walk so she could see the small town. She accepted eagerly, and they passed by Sunless Street, where the tall ageless trees diffused an intoxicating breeze and inter-twined at the top to wrap the long alley with their giant shadow. The birdsong vibrated from the perched king-doms and filled the air with a surreal gaiety. The sun winked through the thick foliage and let its diaphanous rays flood the street, creating the perfect stage for a beautiful morning. Amar had never had a clear idea of happiness but just walking next to Aisha, he was now certain that it was hidden somewhere inside her. He couldn't say if it was in her smile, in her look or in her voice...

He came back in the afternoon and took her to the outskirts where they could climb the small hill that overlooked the city. They sat on top of the hill while Amar told her the story of the huge baobab tree standing majestically in the entrance of the wood. It was reported that the spirits of the town lived in it, and nobody dared to take it down to build the new road for fear of losing their soul. They could see the vast maize fields rustling in the wind and bowing their golden head to the sunset.

"You see the mango trees there behind the cornfields. That was my favorite place. One of the farms used to belong to my grandfather before my uncles sold it. I spent most of my childhood hiding on the top of those trees, playing hide and seek with my little cousins. I miss those times." He said in a nostalgic voice.

"That's beautiful. I am a river girl, and I spent all my childhood near the water. I wish you could come up north one day. Can you swim?" Aisha asked.

"How could I? Growing in a town with no river, no sea, and not even a pool? The only thing I learned as a child was how to steal from people's farms and how to run quickly."

They laughed:

"I could teach you how to swim, how to fish from the river and even how to cook those fish by the riverside." She said while their hands touched accidentally first, but then they slowly reached to each other, staring at the declining sun on the horizon, lost in a universe larger than their own, trying silently to understand that amazing feeling older than their existence...

One morning, Aisha was not waiting for him at her front door as they convened. Amar stayed outside the house, hesitant to go in. He did not want to be an intruder and just stood there like a lamp post. Anguish gnawed at his whole body as he wondered why Aisha did not show up. Tired of waiting, he went home and spent the entire night thinking about her and anticipating the moment he would see her angelic face smiling at him in the distance.

He had never been able to sleep well since he left University, hunting for a job and having to face the contemptuous looks from his family of adoption. He was the only one who made it to college in the family. He had been raised with his four cousins, and they never graduated high school and had always been jealous of him. Ironically, they were now the ones who were earning a living as tailors, carpenters, plumbers, or mechanics. None of those jobs required a high school degree. He was the one who came back from the University with a hollow degree that did not teach him how to use his hands. And the government did not need his general knowledge in science or language arts with no practical skills. His cousins had seen it as revenge for all the humiliations and punishment they went through at school. At least they can take care of themselves, and two of them were already married with kids. He was the one with an undergraduate degree and no penny in his pocket. His situation kept him from sleeping well.

But during those few days, Aisha was the reason that kept him awake all night. Hanging out with her had changed his whole life. For once, he did not think about his desperate situation. He was too busy thinking about her. All he could see were those soft, deep brown eyes staring wondrously at him as if she were struck by the same mysterious lightning that hit his heart at her very first sight, those inviting lips that parted to reveal a delicious smile and a voice that sounded like an announcement from paradise. He liked the way she arranged her beautiful black hair, unbraided but combed neatly, and which perfectly fitted her diamond-shaped face.

Aisha had promised her she would spend the whole summer in the small town. But what if she had an emergency and had to leave without warning him? That would break his heart, and he shook his head in despair and prayed that nothing serious happened to her.

The following morning, when Amar did not see Aisha, he knew something was wrong, and he could not just keep waiting. He decided he should just pay her a random visit and find out. He opened the gate and found an old woman sitting in the front yard and carefully looking after a boiling pot in the open kitchen. He could smell the soft aroma of white rice. The old woman answered his greeting and pointed at the living room when he asked for Aisha. He found her in the company of two other girls her age that politely excused themselves and left the room. Aisha was laying down on the couch, and she tried to sit up, visibly not looking well. But she seemed happy to see him and invited him to take a seat. She explained that she had some fever and did not feel well, probably malaria because it was the season. He felt happy she did not treat him like an intruder, and he felt immediately at home.

But that did not last long. Suddenly, a man in his fifties entered the living room and saw him. He was the chief of the household and was surprised to see him. He was not expecting a visit and frowned when he recognized Amar. Both used to meet sometimes at the neighborhood mosque during the night prayers. That was the only prayer that Amar did at the mosque, even though he was expected to attend five times a day. Amar politely stood up and stretched his hand for a handshake. His hand remained suspended in the air, and instead of a handshake, the old man snapped at him:

"What are you doing in my house, young man?"

He might not know or remember Amar's name, but he seemed to know whose son he was.

"Good morning, papa Musa," Amar said nonetheless, lowering his hand. Then, he added meekly, "Aisha is my friend, and I just stopped by to say hi."

"Are you Amar? The son of the late Balla?" The man suddenly seemed to remember his name.

"Yes, Papa."

"So, I have a question for you: What makes Aisha your friend?" He furrowed his brow and cocked his head. Two red eyes darted at Amar like a furious rooster. Amar wondered how his hat, negligently posed on a corner of his head, did not drop. He felt mortified and did not know how to answer.

"Listen, my son! If you are looking for a friend, a girlfriend or whatever, then this is the wrong house." His fingers were already pointing at the exit door while he stood impatiently.

"Uncle!" Aisha was dumbfounded by her uncle's attitude.

He ignored his niece's pleading voice, and as Amar was heading to the door, he said:

"I guess you have a lot of learning to do about yourself. Go back home and tell your uncle you have been to Papa Musa's house and ask them what they think about it. But to be clear with you, this is no place for you. You are not welcome to my house, and you cannot befriend my niece. Can you understand that?"

And then, to his niece:

"This conversation is not yours, my niece." He roared at her, raising his hand briskly to stop her because Aisha instinctively sprang up as if she wanted to stop Amar from leaving. "This young man knows well what I am talking about. Am I being clear, young man?" Aisha sank into her couch, almost fainting from embarrassment.

Amar opened his mouth to say something, but he could not think of anything to say. He cast a helpless glance at Aisha and left.

He just realized he had entered the wrong house. He never thought about it. For once, he just followed his heart without any second thought, and it had gotten him into that huge embarrassment. That was one of those houses that he would never be welcome. He knew that house and that family, and he was vaguely aware that they were supposed to be above his family in rank. But when he saw Aisha, his heart did not let his mind process the facts. Of course, he should know better. All he could feel now was anger and confusion. Anger for falling for the wrong person. But can he blame his own heart for wanting somebody? He was confused because instead of love, he felt hatred brewing inside of him. Aisha's uncle might just be another victim of century-old ignorant beliefs and tradition. Yet, it didn't make it less hurtful. For him, that man would always stand for the person that stood against his happiness in the most barbaric manner.

They were said to be one of those noble families where people like him could never pretend to date a girl. His grandparents, his parents had been their servants or slaves. They were needed in there only when there was a big party so that they could do the cooking, the serving, and the clean-up, and sing the family glory and be offered a few coins in exchange. They had to show how they were grateful, how their own parents had been good servants to their grandparents and parents. Why would things be different with him?

Of course, he had been to school and more and more, the gap had been filled by education. But it works only when you are a success story or a self-made person. If you become rich overnight, you will be welcome in any family, whatever your ancestral history. Money will make everybody sing your glory and welcome you in any house. But he was just a college dropout with no money, no job, no bright future. He was not even welcome in his own family. Why would someone else do it?

He returned to his empty, monotonous, and sad life. But now he had to avoid 'Aisha's Street'. With what happened, he felt humiliated and could not look her in the eyes again. Her uncle had belittled him and had shown him that he was not even fit to be friends with a decent girl. He had to suck in his desire as well as his dreams.

He had once found refuge in studies and school, where he felt it was the only place in the world where there seemed to be some equalities. They all wore the same uniforms, sat at the same desk, learned the same subject and yet... after school, life goes back to the old-fashioned circle of social inequalities and injustice. The poor go back to their huts, the middle class goes back to their brick-made houses, the noble goes back to being condescending, and the 'griot' or the 'casted', to being humble and low profile.

From that day on, he could never walk in that part of the street again. Every morning, he would wake up early, as usual, take a shower and do his morning prayer. He would drink a glass of water. He could not remember the last time he had had a breakfast. The only meals that were shared in the family were lunch and dinner. They were served in three big bowls: one for the men, one for the women and another for the kids. Each adult in the house took care of his own breakfast, and he could not afford it. Bread and milk were expensive. Forget about eggs. He would walk to the house gate and, leaning on the wall, he would helplessly peer into the distance, fearing and hoping at the same time that Aisha would show up.

Sometimes, basking in the morning sun with closed eyes, he daydreamed about going with her in some very distant land where only love prevailed, not the backward and retrograded idea of relationships based on rank and social prestige. A land where they would be free to love and live happily without having to worry about who their father or mother was. A land where a heart is a heart, free to love and be loved. A land where a person is a person, not a half person or inferior or superior. For him, 'Aisha's Street' had become a 'no way', and he would take the opposite way if he had to go somewhere and make a huge detour, no matter how long.

He decided he had to move to the capital. He would do any job to survive; car wash, cleaning, tutoring, anything that could take him out of that misery but also that could take him away from Aisha. A girl he could never love, but also a girl he could never stop thinking about. He had no idea when, or if, he would ever come back to his native town. He lost hope of finding a job, now that he lost hope even for love, he had no reason to stick to a place that denied him everything. He would head for the capital, never to come or look back.

And for the last time, he thought he should pass by 'Aisha's Street'. He would not enter the house, of course. He would just go that way for one last time and bid a silent farewell to the girl who made his heart beat so loud. For the first time, he could hear his heart speak to him. His heart crying his longing and desire. He felt hurt. He felt even more hurt as he thought he had detected in her eyes the same amount of yearning to love and be loved. He wished nothing had ever happened, and nothing would ever happen. But he could sadly realize that it was too late. He was already in love with Aisha.

At the very moment he passed by Aisha's front door for the last time, a young boy ran after him and handed him a letter. He almost refused to take it, and the boy insisted and told him it was from Aisha. He took the letter and rushed home. He could not help shaking as he read it:

Once again, Fall is over, and the leaves
Of the trees sway gently along the windy streets.
Hope and dream slowly drop from my heart.

Winter will be around, and with it, loneliness and sorrow
    will make me
turn over and over in my bed, my hands groping in the
    shadows
for your missing face... so present in my dreams

And Spring will come and the roses, in the middle of the
    corridor,
Will spread their petals to the maze of your heart,
    beautiful and pure

And I will behold in the distance, sinking in my
    loneliness.

With you, no matter what, life promised to be always
    sunny.
Blessed is the summer that brought you to me
Those days that will count for thousands. Forever.

But fate with its dark wing spread despair and
Buried our hopes in the muddy cloud of ignorance
And into the sullen silence sank our world

I will seek for you into the darkness
Hoping you will take my hand and together
We will walk down the sunny street

And over our head the light of our love
Will mingle with the sunshine to make
The world brighter someday...

He had dropped the letter as if he had felt a burning in
his hands. His heart had beaten so hard that he felt out of
breath and rushed to the water jug and drank a big mug
of water. He regained his breath but not his mind. He felt
it was not real and hurried back to his room. He glanced,
and the letter was lying on the ground, very real. It was
neither an illusion nor a dream. He read it again, this time
more attentively, and lay down on his bed, and the only
thing he could think of was... "She loves me too... She loves
me too..." He kept saying.

He should never have kept that letter. It stood as an
umbilical link between him and the past, between him and
Aisha. Now it was time for him to get rid of it because

Christine had appeared in his life, and he had the impression that the curtain was drawn on a part of his life, and on the other side, he saw a reflection of the sun dancing joyfully to show him the way to happiness. He walked to the kitchen and lit the gas stove. A blue flame erupted, and for the last time, he glared at the letter and directed it to the flame. He held it solemnly and looked thoughtfully at the piece of paper that crackled and writhed as it became red, black, and finally white. Before his eyes, part of his heart turned to ashes. He turned off the stove, considered the ashes he had collected from a small piece of paper, then poured the contents into the kitchen sink and opened the tap with a nonchalant gesture. He had just cremated part of his past.

CHAPTER
SIX

Christine's apartment complex was perched on a hillside that provided luxuriant vegetation at its bottom, with fresh scents pouring into the crisp air to envelop the quiet and peaceful city. A bird's eye view revealed nature in all its splendor where air, solid and liquid combined their talent to present the picture of life, immense and incommensurable. From the bottom of the hills, one could admire the sumptuous architecture that stood against the sky, recalling one of those picturesque paintings made on a life-size scale, the background setting of which changes according to the seasons of the year and the times of the day. A row of pine trees stood in sentinels to protect the peaceful lake, and in the summer, a few solitary canoeists rowed in silence and fishermen, scattered along the cemented edges, waited patiently for the poles or trout to bite the hook. The pine trees provided access to a bushy wood where balsam firs, hemlocks, and giant maples shot up vigorously to gain access to daylight. They proudly displayed their majestic foliage, which sang with the wind the hymn of life, and on warm mornings, deers, satiated with maple leaf and smelling of the balm of wildflowers, could be seen shuffling on the hill on the lookout for the first rays of the sun. During the fall, various colored leaves, ranging from red, yellow, and orange, ornated the ground to pay tribute to mother nature before being buried during the winter under a shroud of snow. In spring, everything revived and renewed the legendary pact of life that linked the earth and the sky.

Amar sat towards the window and admired the golden vault of the sun, which was about to retreat in his unearthly cottage.

"It is a beautiful view, isn't it?"

"It is beautiful. I love nature. I did not have much luck with my family, and nature was my only refuge. I went to the wood a lot and spent the most peaceful moments of my life on my grandfather's farm."

"Ah, a lover of nature," she says tenderly.

"Let's say that nature had adopted me." He continued in a nostalgic voice. "It was a shelter and a refuge for me because I had no one else. So, the only times I felt happy was when I escaped from my hellish home to make it to the paradise of nature."

Amar loved playing with little Josh while Christine was busy in the kitchen. Like all kids his age, Josh loved toy cars and would bring them and proudly display them to Amar. He would also urge Amar to tell him stories about animals. Amar had already told him all the classic western African tales he knew about the smart rabbit and the naïve hyena, the story about animals in the jungle and their king, the lion. He had to make up more stories because Josh constantly wanted to hear new ones. He kept his mother's regular features but must have inherited his brown eyes and tanned skin from his father. Amar liked to see the little boy's chubby face split into a delicious smile, his soft eyes twinkling with joy, listening to his jerky and contagious laugh, which distilled his own sorrows and relieved his pains. He had never known that the joys of a child could be so beneficent.

He would have liked to go to Christine's house every night after work and stay there all night. However, he lived on the other side of the city, far from these peaceful and quiet suburbs. He was dreaming about when he could move and live with Christine. Everything happened very quickly between him and the young woman. They appreciated the moments spent together, and each reveled in hearing the other speak, while the great difference between their origins and their cultures sharpened their curiosity, filled their ignorance, and brought them more together. Christine liked the positive vibe that Amar brought into the apartment. His presence and radiance shattered the monotony of the place, sparked the apartment with life and filled the void that prevented it from being a normal home.

Amar had never felt so appreciated in his life. Christine's apartment seemed to him like a haven of peace where he forgot all the pain and fatigue. He felt light and transported into a strange world, and sometimes he had to make a lot of effort to get back to reality and recognize that he was not dreaming. He was wondering whether his soul had not traveled in another body and that he was still the same person. He cracked his knuckles; an old habit he had. He knew he was not dreaming. The path of life can lead to the most unusual situation, and sometimes it can take you to a place that even a dream will not.

Tired of playing, little Josh ended up falling asleep on the sofa. Christine, returning from the kitchen, glanced tenderly at the sleeping toddler:

"You two get along so well."

"Josh is so adorable. I could spend a whole day with him without getting bored." He said, thinking that he would have loved to be the father of this wonderful boy.

He could not help dreaming of founding a family. The idea crossed his mind, and instead of getting excited, he was suddenly filled with fear and unanswered questions. How would Christine react if he shared his intention with her? He knew she was not close to her parents, but what would be their reactions if they found out that their daughter had a black boyfriend? He had heard about some of those interracial relationships that did not end well, and he could not imagine himself being the center of conflict. He could not help thinking about Aisha, who had the same skin color as him, and that had not prevented him from being kicked out like an animal. He shook his head and tried to think positively. He decided to join Christine in the kitchen:

"What good stuff are you making?" He asked as he approached her.

"Just a little vegetable omelet. Nothing out of the ordinary. But you are going to like it. I promise."

"Of course, I will love everything that comes from you... except..."

"Pork? Do not worry about that. I don't cook pork."

"How can you read my mind? I think that is the definition of a soul mate, when one begins to think, and the other finishes his thought."

"It was not as difficult as you think because we were talking about food, and I already knew you do not eat pork. But on the other hand, you are right. I think I can read your thoughts."

"And what can you read right now?"

"With the way you are looking at me, it is not hard to guess." She said in a teasing tone and alluringly rolled her eyes.

"Maybe you are right... Let us see if that is true."

Amar drew her against him. He loved the soft feel of her silky hair on his cheek, smelling her discreet and exquisite scent while tenderly hugging her. He placed his lips on hers, and the world, like a big giant candy, melted gently. Christine closed her eyes and let herself be carried away by the magic of those captivating moments. She wanted to roll herself up like a liana around this slender and muscular body. His brawny arms wrapped her in a delicious grip, and she snuggled up even more, feeling overwhelmed by a comfort and coolness she had never known.

Amar made her feel beautiful and secure, a feeling she had lost a long time ago. His courtesy, respect and delicate manner had won her. She did not regret getting to know him more, and with him, the cruel and material world dissipated to give way to a sweet and peaceful universe. His presence changed her apartment into paradise, and for nothing in the world, she would not let that happiness escape her. She just wanted him to stay and never leave.

———

Amar heard the apartment door open and knew that it was Demba who had just returned because Gora was already in bed. Demba was on his own schedule and could come in and out at any time depending on the phone call from customers who sometimes worked late at night. He never turned off his phone, and Amar wondered how he managed to not sleep on the steering wheel of his minivan taxi. He heard him take a shower, and then he would usually do his ablutions and pray before going to bed for a few hours. Demba almost never slept. Amar waited for a while. He knew Demba's habits well and wanted to talk to him. He wanted to wait until he finished doing his evening prayers. He guiltily found that he had missed many prayers most recently. He was supposed to 'pay off' all his missed prayers of the day because of his job, but more and more he was skipping them. Usually, that was why he would rush home after work to take a shower and do his prayer, eat something, and go to sleep. Now, the first thing he often thought about after work was going to see Christine. And when he left late at night, he was too tired to think about praying.

He was startled at the idea of going down the wrong path so easily. He got up and went to the bathroom, made his ablutions, and joined Demba, who was standing on the praying mat in the corner of the living room. He stood next to him and let himself be guided through the different stages of the prayers. It was like the old days when he had just arrived in this country, when every night they stood side by side to pray together.

When they finished, Demba glanced at him. It had been so long since they had prayed together, and Demba immediately knew that something had happened. Before

Amar even opened his mouth, he turned to him:

"Why do you honor me with your presence tonight? It has been so long since we had time to pray together."

"You're right, big brother." He always called him that way. "Because of our hectic life, we end up losing the good old habits."

"That is not a good reason, my dear. I have lived here longer than you and Gora, and I have never lost my habits. It is hard, but it is not impossible."

"I would try to do better because you are a role model for us. But, big brother," he said after a brief silence, "I came to talk to you about something, and I would need your advice."

Demba had no idea and wondered what it could be. He sighed and hoped it was not something serious. Amar rapidly reassured him when he saw his concerned face:

"Actually, it is nothing serious. It is a little late and I do not want to hold you back too much, but this is the situation I am in right now, and since you are family to me, I think I should tell you about it. I have met a girl, and our relationship is getting more and more serious. To be honest, I like her very much. The years are passing fast, and I thought it was time for me to consider getting married. Besides, I am a Muslim, and I don't think it is appropriate for me to date a woman without any serious purpose."

Demba's lips moved silently as he was saying some silent incantations. He always ended his meditation that way. He then put away his praying beads and faced Amar:

"I am glad you talked to me about it." He said with a sigh of relief. "You are still young, and it is so easy to make mistakes." He seemed to think for a few seconds and then asked:

"As far as I know, you have not been with that woman long enough to know her well. Have you talked to her? Have you ever met her family?"

Amar had to admit that there were still so many unanswered questions. As he was trying to talk about Christine, he could feel the reluctance of Demba, who was shrinking into himself. When he realized that Amar was talking about a young white woman, the disapproval was more and more visible on his face. Amar felt he had to deal with the situation with nonchalance to reduce the tension in the air.

"I haven't talked to her yet about it. Also, she is not on good terms with her parents. I just thought I should talk to you first before anything else."

"I have never met that woman. I don't know her, so it would be hard for me to make any judgment or give some advice. But I would be very cautious about a woman I don't share the same culture or belief... Those are important in a relationship. Maybe you should take your time and learn more about her before making an important decision. Also, what about her? Are you sure this is not just a crush and that she is taking it as a serious relationship?"

"I feel she cares deeply about me, and it could be just beneficial for both of us to consider a long-term relationship."

"The only way to find out is to have a serious talk with her but... Amar, have you ever considered a woman from your own culture?"

Amar felt as if the question was a silent reproach from Demba. It was his way of telling him to get away from that relationship. He pursued:

"There are a lot of beautiful women here that share your culture and your beliefs. I know many who would be more than happy to marry a man like you, serious and hardworking."

Amar did not like the way the conversation was heading because he realized that Demba was trying to dissuade him. He had not come to tell him to introduce him to other women or to choose for him. He had already chosen Christine. He knew that what he was about to say would disappoint Demba, but he wanted to make it clear.

"I apologize, big brother, but I do not think I need to meet anybody. I feel that my heart has already chosen, and I love this woman whom I am currently dating." He said, trying to sound as polite as possible.

"Young brother, you are old enough to make your own decisions. But to be honest with you, I strongly advise you not to marry a girl who is not of your culture. Get married to one of our women. There are a lot of them here who want husbands. What you are currently experiencing might be just a momentary feeling, but marriage is forever. And there are some hurdles that even love cannot overcome. Sooner or later, those hurdles will bring down the love or passion that binds you, and it will be even worse if you have confused carnal desire and love."

Amar did not expect to be lectured by Demba. He remained silent, and when he thought about it, he had not even told Christine about his plans. But it was important for him to pick up some advice from his friends before making a final decision. He thought there was no point trying to convince Demba. He just wanted to have his point of view and prepare him for the decision he was about to make. But also, he knew the final decision did not even depend on him. He would have to talk to Christine, and everything would hinge on her. But at his level, he had already made up his mind, and as if he did not want Demba to read his thoughts, he deemed it wise to stop the discussion:

"I have heard your words, big brother, and I would take that into account. Now, it is getting late. Thank you for the advice. We will talk about it later. Good night." And he took leave and returned to his room.

Laying on his bed, Amar thought of what Demba had told him. He realized that there was some truth to what he had said. He even felt overwhelmed by a feeling of doubt. He had found that his relationship with Christine impacted his actions. He sometimes forgot to pray, things he had never experienced before. He felt that the more he became involved in this relationship, the more he lost part of himself, of his convictions. But at the same time, it was the only way to find some balance in his life, for lack of a better solution. He felt that he had already gone too far with Christine, and he could no longer turn his life around. After all, his religion allowed him to marry a person of different faith or belief, and from that perspective, he can at least find a solution to part of the problem.

CHAPTER
SEVEN

It was no longer a secret to the rest of the restaurant that Amar was dating Christine. First, he had feared that it might cost him his job. It had never occurred to his mind that he would one day mix work and pleasure. He was so consumed by his tough and ungrateful job, which did not allow him any rest nor time for pleasure. His life was dull and was all about work. Everybody in the restaurant seemed to mind their own business as he and Christine were not the first employees to date and would not be the last ones. The only person he felt was looking at him with an evil eye was John, the assistant manager. He did not take well the relationship between Amar and Christine, especially after that one had rejected him. He would not give him food anymore, even if he asked for it. He would pretend he had forgotten, or he was busy, and the food was coming, and it would never come.

Abdu seemed to encourage him, although Amar had the weird feeling that he was not being sincere. Amar knew his co-worker had a wicked personality, and the more he pushed him in the relationship, the more cautious he felt he had to be. But also, he knew his heart was already trapped and even if he wanted to avoid any turbulence along the way, he could not. It was too late for him to be rescued. Christine already filled his mind and heart, and there was no more room for reason and common sense.

"Did you know you can get your green card if you marry her?" Abdu once asked him.

"I heard so. But I would not want to marry her just to get a green card."

"You are so naïve, my friend. Remember what I told you. Women fall in love just for a short period. You have been in this country forever, and this is the only chance to get your green card. It is time for your star to shine, and if you let it fade away, you will stay in the shadow forever. Believe me, I have been here long enough, and I know what I am talking about."

He admitted that he had a lot to win if Christine accepted to marry him, but he also wanted to reject the idea that it was only for a green card. He loved her and asking for her hand was the right thing to do. But the big question in his mind was how he could deal with that matter without scaring Christine away. He was very conscious about the relatively short time they had spent together, but as they say in his country: 'If you plan to do something good, you should act fast'. Bad things can happen so quickly and ruin your plan. Although he didn't fully trust Abdu, he could not help asking him for some advice:

"Don't you think it is too early to think about

marriage?"

"It is never too early to propose, my friend. Have you ever watched 'Marriage at First Sight'?" Abdu asked him.

"I believe I saw it a couple of times on TV." He said.

"Well, if people can propose without even seeing each other, you surely can propose if you have been seeing each other for over a month," Abdu stated.

"I think you are right. I must admit I thought about it, and I even discussed it with Demba, my roommate."

"You see, my friend, I knew you were smart, and you were working on something," Abdu said as if he were talking to himself. "And what did he say?"

"You know Demba. He is so conservative. He thinks I should choose a girl from my country."

"And that is the reason he had been here for so long without paper. I just think you should learn from the mistakes of others, so you won't have to spend all your life without any opportunity. And as I told you, it is about time you took things seriously in your hands." He advised.

"Thank you for being so positive. That's very helpful."

Amar was so surprised Abdu was giving such good advice. That was definitely not like him. Usually, his favorite game was to backbite at people. It could be anybody from co-workers to the members of the African community. He did not care as long as he could find something bad to say. But presently, he was telling him exactly what he wanted to hear. Amar thought he had been misjudging his co-worker a little bit and felt guilty about thinking he was jealous of him. He was going to act fast and not let Christine slip away from him.

———

Amar and Christine were sitting in the playground area of a nearby mall and were watching little Josh happily strolling between the toys. This was one of the rare moments they happened to be off together, and they wanted to enjoy it. Amar could not help dreaming about having his own family. He wished he were the father of the little boy.

"I heard you were having some issues with John. What was it about?" He was taken from his daydream by Christine.

"He was trying to have me clean and mop the kitchen while I was drowning at dish land. And of course, I could not be both places at the same time, and he was being impatient and was yelling at me."

"And you yelled back at him? People say that was the first time they saw you that angry."

"Because I was hungry too, and as the singer said, 'A hungry man is an angry man'." He tried to joke. "But to be honest with you, I think he is jealous of our relationship. He is being so mean to me recently. He lets me starve and never gives me a break. I suspect it is because of what is going on between you and me."

And he added softly:

"I heard he tried to date you."

"Yes, but he is not my type. And he is still running after me. You are probably right. Just be careful... I don't want you to get into trouble."

"Don't worry about that, Christine. I am not an essential worker here, and I know a lot of restaurant owners who are looking for dishwashers." He shrugged with resignation.

"Yeah, but still be careful. People can act crazy out of

jealousy sometimes."

He felt a little worried. Christine was right. There were so many crazy people out there, and sometimes it was people you suspect the least that could be capable of the worst. But the joy he secretly felt overcame his worries. Christine really cared about him. He never felt so appreciated in his life. The fact she chose him over John meant a lot to him. John was not only a charming young man, but he was also his boss. But everyone in the restaurant knew that he was a player. Amar took it as a sign that Christine was more into a long-term relationship. A feeling of confidence invaded him, and he reached out to her and patted her hand. He felt like pulling her closer and hugging her, but they were in a public place, and he could never do that.

"I appreciate so much you worry about me. It means you care about me."

"I do care about you, Amar." She nudged him with her elbow and smiled at him.

He thought about his plan, about his discussion with Abdu, and he felt like going down on his knees and proposing to her. But he knew it was not that simple. Whereas in Africa, everything would depend on the parents' consent, the main hurdle for him would be Christine herself. She seemed to be content about how their relationship was going, and though they learned to appreciate each other more and connect on a deeper level, he was not sure if she was willing to go as far as getting married. The only way he could find out was to ask her. And with Abdu's words in mind, he was not even sure if, with time, their relationship was going to grow or weaken. And that added to his confusion about when it would be the right moment to make a move.

Little Josh came running to them as they got up to continue their walk through the mall...

Nick, Mike and Tony were sitting outside on the porch of Mike's house.

"I just got a job in a McDonald's, guys," Tony said hesitantly.

He was somewhat dreading the reaction of Mike, who had never hidden his dislike for a regular job. A little silence ensued, and he added:

"Besides, they need another assistant," he added, avoiding Mike's eyes.

"I think I will apply," Nick said. "Now that I am not going to school anymore. I will have to work a little. Besides, I think Mom's about to kick me out. All hell broke loose when I got expelled from school."

They could see the cars speeding down Grand River Avenue and their newfound game to have some fun was to count the number of luxury cars that passed along the Avenue. They would challenge one another on who would count the most cars. They had to be keen-eyed and be the first to spot a luxury car from a distance.

"If you want to spend the rest of your life behind a counter selling burgers for eight dollars an hour, that's your business. I want to be rich – and fast." Mike absent-mindedly told them. He then shouted before the others could see it. "Red Chevrolet Corvette! That is six for me." He had good eyes and was ahead of the others.

"I am going to tell you the truth, guys. I do not just want to count them. I want to own them. This Corvette

Chevrolet can run 180 miles per hour, and it costs no less than fifty thousand dollars. For me to have one like that, I need fast and easy money. And it is not the kind of job you are talking about that can get me one." He contemptuously added.

"Stop dreaming," Tony stuttered. "I do not know any talent you got. You are not good at basketball; you are not a rap star. How do you think you will get rich overnight?"

"Don't be an idiot. You know PJ, right? He is barely older than us, and he already has his own car and his own apartment. What talents do you think he got?"

"Apart from hustling and selling drugs…"

"Don't say no more. For people who have no talent or qualification, that is the only way to get rich. In fact, I have already had a good talk with Malcolm. He is PJ's boss. And he says he will holler at me."

"How did you get in touch?" Nick said. "Did you tell him about us?"

"I have my connections but, in that business, you must zip your lips if you don't want trouble. I will tell him about you when the time is right. For now, just be ready. I would need help when something is up."

"I will find a job just for a while. I do not plan to spend my whole life standing behind a counter." Nick said.

"You two will get me in trouble," Tony said. "Life would be so simple if we stick to ourselves, find a quiet little job, and stay out of trouble."

Mike interrupted him:

"Because you think life is simple. Make no mistake, my friend; life is not meant to be simple. Men are worse than fish. You eat or you get eaten. I want to be a big fish. And for that, you will have to eat the small fish to survive. If you want to be the small fish, well... too bad for you."

He suddenly became silent when he saw in the distance a man who had parked his taxi in front of the gas station on the other side of the road.

"I hate him." He murmured as if he were talking to herself.

"Who?" Inquired Nick as he followed his friend's gaze.

His eyes were fixed on the slender figure of the African cab driver who always came to that gas station to refill his tank:

"I can recognize the cab of that stupid man from a mile away."

"What did this gentleman do to you?" Tony asked.

"I can't stand him. He is always around with his old beater. A few years back, he had forced me to give back twenty dollars that some idiot had dropped. I was behind the lady, and he was behind me. When I picked up the money and was about to pocket it, the silly guy asked me to give the money back to the lady. Why did he have to interfere? That was not his money. All he had to do was take care of his own business. He had literally humiliated me. Since then, I hated him, and he will pay for that."

"You were wrong to want to keep that money," said Tony. He seemed to have more common sense than his two friends.

"It was not my fault that the stupid lady dropped her money in the street," Mike said angrily. "Twenty dollars by then would have made my day. I did not care if it was right or wrong. I needed money, and it was God sent, and the foolish man intervened... Well, to come back to our plan, if you want to make it to the top, you will have to work hard to earn it. These people don't play games. They need tough guys, not cowards."

They spent much of their days sitting in front of the porch, playing on their telephones, and chatting.

"Now that I'm going to have a paycheck, the first thing I'm going to do is buy me a good Xbox and invite Yvonne out," Tony said.

"I want to buy a gun; it is more fun," Nick said.

"Hell yeah!" yelled Mike. "Guns! That is what we need, buddy."

He already had a wild look in his eyes and stared at a point as if he were already holding a gun in his hand and was targeting an invisible enemy.

"When we get started, we will work on some strategies. It will take a lot of work to have the boss's trust." He said with a voice that sounded like he was already in charge.

"Got you, bro," Nick replied in a committed voice.

CHAPTER
EIGHT

Amar was thrilled. He had been able to leave the restaurant early, like every beginning of the week. Mondays and Tuesdays were his favorite days of the week because the restaurant was not busy on those days, and he could leave early and go to Christine's apartment. Usually, customers started to pick up from Wednesday to the rest of the week and the peak days were Friday and Saturday. On those days, he left late but also exhausted.

He had been dating Christine for a while now, and he could not keep postponing his plan. He thought proposing was the right thing to do because, as a practicing Muslim, he had no right to live with a woman without marrying her or at least having the intention of marrying her. He had had some random conversation with her, and she had expressed her preference for unconventional relationships. She was not against the idea of long-term relationships, but for her, people could be happy without the burden of social conventions. He believed her past must have something to do with her convictions, and he felt it was his job to convince her. He was optimistic with all the love and complicity growing between them.

After they hung out and ate dinner together, he solemnly went to his knees in front of her, took her hand, and pulled out a ring from his pocket. He had secretly bought a white ring encrusted with small golden tips. He was shaking and nervous. He fought hard to get rid of that lump of emotion that obstructed his throat and prevented him from speaking. In his confusion, he did not know if he had taken out the ring at the right time. He had tried, with no success, to remember a little speech that he had rehearsed a few times, and all he wanted suddenly was to get rid of the ring, which was becoming heavier and heavier for his shaking hand:

"I love you, Christine," he said under a heavy breath. "I'd like to ask you if you will marry me."

She flinched, taken aback by that request that was so unexpected. Amar moved one of his hands, and Christine panicked at the thought that he would place the ring on her finger. She was in a deep struggle inside because she didn't want to hurt him but also, she knew she was not ready to accept an engagement ring at that moment in her life. Every woman would have jumped with joy and excitement when a man made that kind of move, and although she was overcome with emotion, she could not say yes. Instead of stretching her finger to let him put the ring on, she grabbed Amar's hand, her eyes suddenly full of tears and instantly joined him on her knees. She felt touched by his kind gesture but could not accept the offer.

"Ooh, that is so sweet of you, Amar. This is so unexpected... But I think we need more time. We need to know each other better and take our time before committing to such a serious issue." She said hesitantly.

She spoke cautiously because she was at a loss what to say and had to think hard about what was coming out of her mouth. It was so easy to hurt somebody in such a situation. A misplaced word could hurt more than a blow in the head.

"Christine, we have been together for some time now. It might be a short time, but that was enough for me to know you are the right woman for me. I have no doubt about that." He felt a little embarrassed by her hesitation, but he had already proposed, and it was too late to back up. Christine was silent and avoided looking at him. He felt she was having some interior conflict, and he had to push more.

"Honey, I'm not even asking you to make up your mind today or tomorrow. Take all your time to think. All I am asking you is to give me a chance, and I'll wait as long as you want. Please, all I am asking is a chance..." He pleaded, hoping to convince her.

"I feel honored... but this is so unexpected," she said in a weak voice.

"I have been through a lot, honey. I am just not ready for that yet. We have everything we need to be happy." She went on in a brittle voice drenched with emotion and bad memories. "I have seen my mom go through hell under the pretense she was in a marital relationship. I personally went through relationships that had left some scars on me. And the idea of marriage just scares me right now. I am so sorry, Amar."

Amar was already regretting his act, realizing that Christine was not ready for such a commitment. He felt like something solid they had built together was suddenly crumbling down, leaving him with a feeling of despair.

"I am not those persons you are talking about, and you are not your mom, Christine!" He said a little loudly and was surprised by his own voice. He wanted to shake off the wrong idea 'that marriage equals failure' out of her mind, out of her body. She seemed to have worn those ideas inside her like an incurable disease.

"Everything in life has a brighter and darker side, Christine. Let's focus on the brighter side of life." He was desperately pleading with her to consider her position.

"Don't let bad memories ruin your life. I feel tortured by seeing you every day, loving you and not being able to ask for your hand. I feel so incomplete right now. I must confess that my religion imposes marriage on me, and I find myself in an awkward situation. Marriage, or not, will not change my feelings for you. But it bothers me a lot not to be able to take our relationship to the next level." He did not know what else to say and stared blankly at the uncertain path their relationship was about to take.

"I wish we could just live the present and let the future decide..." Christine tried to comfort him.

What he dreaded the most was happening. He had not banked on Christine's refusal to commit, and he felt ridiculous. He had thought it was a possibility, but the more he tried, the more he felt that chance eluding him. Fortunately, he had not revealed his plan to his friends Demba and Gora. Otherwise, his embarrassment would have been even bigger. He wanted to make sure he knew which direction the relationship was going. Now, the question was, what could he expect from Christine? Could he hope their relationship would grow with time and end up in the direction he wanted, or would it just fade out like a simple love affair? And how long would he be able to keep such a relationship without alienating himself and becoming another person? He was about to reach his objective of settling down and having a normal family life. That had always been his biggest dream. He had hoped he would find the feeling of love and security his own country had denied him, here on this side of the world. All of a sudden, his dream was eluding him.

The idea of marriage always brought up in Christine's mind the image of her parents, trapped in an unhappy relationship and just staying together to save appearances. She had never believed in marriage. By trying to escape the toxic environment from her family, she fell into the arms of a drug-addicted boyfriend. After tragedy had struck, she had to go through another bad relationship. All the turmoil she had gone through had carved in her mind the unbreakable yearning to preserve her freedom in any future relationship.

As a young girl, she had almost believed in the mirage of marriage, which promised the illusion of happiness. But as she grew up, she was convinced that it brought more suffering than happiness. She had seen a glimmer of hope with Amar. She just wished she could live her life with Amar without having to marry him. Marriage had destroyed her mother. And without knowing it, Amar was asking her to return to that somber territory she had witnessed in the past.

Gora was watching his friend and could spot traces of an inner struggle from his tired features and haggard look. He could not understand the reason for this apparent agitation. Usually, he was the one who could not control his mood swings but not Amar, whom he had always known as serene and placid. He hated to see his friend that way, and suddenly he felt the urge to make him relax and give him advice because when it came to girls, he was the expert of the house.

He thought it was good for Amar to have a girlfriend, and as far as he was concerned, it was even better for his health. He knew he could never live like Amar and Demba because he had too much energy, and he'd rather spend it chasing women than getting into other kinds of trouble. That was the only reason he did not go crazy in this country. Amar was a romantic and introverted person. Besides, he was too spiritual. If he were a Catholic, he could have been an excellent priest because he had always wondered how he could abstain for so long when there were so many women around, who would be more than happy to be chased and feel desired.

He was looking at his friend with a mixture of pity and amusement because of the irony of the situation. Anybody else would be happy and excited to have a new girlfriend, but Amar looked confused because of the same reason. Besides, how beautiful and classy that girl looked! He had shown him her picture on his phone, and if he had been in Amar's shoes, he would break up with all the plain-looking women he was chasing and be a good, faithful man. Amar did not just realize how lucky he was, and he was determined to let him know:

"You see, my friend, right now, you should be the

happiest man in the world. You just won the whole package with that girl. Besides, when are you going to invite her to come and eat with us? Now I am looking up to you, my friend. I did not know you had such good taste in women. My god! Did you take a good look at that woman? She looks like a whole package, my friend!"

Gora felt he was in his favorite element. He was obsessed with women and loved to talk about them. He was the only one to bring them into the apartment, and for once, someone other than him seemed interested in them. He was thrilled because it would allow him to talk about his favorite topic to keep away stress and boredom.

"It is more complicated than you think, Gora. Christine is a good girl, but she is not ready for marriage."

"But who is talking about marriage, my dear? She is right not to think about marriage. It is about having fun, enjoying what life has to offer today because we do not know what tomorrow will be."

"But you know that we are Muslims, and that is not a good thing."

Gora looked at him. He was stunned.

"So, you mean all this time that you are staying without a woman. It's because of religion? How naïve of you. Look, you are no more religious than I am. I pray like you. I fast like you. And you know why? It is because I am a man, and I am supposed to commit sins... And for your information, prayers and fasting are meant to wash sins away..." Gora reminded him.

"You already admit that it is a sin. So, it is better not to do so."

"The guardian angels God hired to forgive men must hate you right now. You send them directly to unemployment because that is their job to forgive the humans who must repent through prayers, fasting and other good deeds. Wake up, my man... and besides, the lady will dump you if she knows that you are so old-fashioned. She must have regretted choosing you over your manager." Gora said sarcastically.

"I feel confused right now...." Amar confessed.

"Relax, my friend. Life is short, and there is only one life. Don't tell me that all the time you have been together, you have only been sitting by her politely talking about marriage and religion. Sometimes women want actions, not words. By the way, have you?"

He wanted to tease his friend out of his boring and barricaded world. Amar stayed silent. He felt embarrassed because he was not used to talking about women with his roommate. His guilty smile did not escape his friend, who gushed out of his seat all excited...

"That's what I am talking about!"

Amar looked away while Gora approached and patted him on his shoulders:

"You see, my friend. That is all we have got in this life. In this crazy country, if you do not do drugs, you don't drink, you don't smoke, and you deprive yourself of women, you'll lose your mind. Go ahead! Have fun! Enjoy life!"

"I feel like I have fallen into a trap. The more I enjoy it, the more guilty I feel. I just wish things were different. I don't feel like myself anymore, and I don't even have the strength to back out.

"The reason is simple: there is no backing out. You want to deny yourself happiness, and this is against nature. By denying nature to express itself, you are causing self-inflicted pain. You do not deserve that; she does not deserve that either…" Gora stated.

The door of the apartment opened, and Demba entered. He waved and went to his room in a hurry, he was always running after the missed prayers, and the first thing he did when he set foot in the apartment was to catch up with his prayers before doing anything else.

"Hi, big brother," Gora said, waving back at him. "Did you talk to him about it?" He said in a low voice.

"I did not go into all the details with him, but he thinks that it is not a good idea. He even told me that if I want to get married, he can put me in touch with some good women who are looking for husbands." Amar whispered.

"Of course, birds of a feather flock together. You two have the same backward ideas. Anyway, I told you what I think, but you should know what you want, and the final decision will depend on you." Gora said.

Amar had a hard time accepting Gora's views, but it allowed him to see things in a different light and made him relax a little. However, he had refrained from telling him the whole story because he felt ashamed of what happened with Christine. Without realizing it, Gora had sided with the young woman because, for him too, marriage was not the most important thing in a relationship.

Two floors above that of Amar and his friends, muffled screams and blows could be heard. Seku was once again playing his favorite game: abusing his wife. It was a way for him to get rid of the rage that was embedded in him since he lost his job. He used violence to compensate for the emptiness and monotony of endless days. Fatima faced her fate, unable to leave her children and forced to face her husband's violence. She was exhausted and emaciated because she barely ate and worked herself to death, just so that her children could eat and dress.

Every morning she left the apartment with the youngest to go to Alima's salon and return in the evening to take care of her family. After a hard day's work, she then had to make sure to cook in case the food was finished. And not only did she have to take care of her children, but she also had to hand some of her money to Seku. She was in trouble if she did not make money. Her husband would assume she was hiding her earnings from him and would start being loud and cursing at everybody in the household. And once Seku started cursing, it would always end up with the beating of his wife. No matter what Fatima did to appease him, he would always end up accusing her of cheating, of hiding money from him or just not cooking the meal the right way or at the right time...

Fatima suffered the violence of her husband with great stoicism, refusing to scream to spare the ears of the kids, the only treasures and joys that life had ever entrusted her with. The children, under their mother's instructions, always took refuge in their small room, which they locked. They did not even dare turn on the light, and their big, scared eyes watched through the door lock their abusive father ill-treating their mother. They huddled and comforted one another in the dark, shaking, and smothering their tears as they cried in silence.

Fatima chose to stay because she had been raised to endure the torments of marriage. Her parents had advised her to stand whatever difficulties might occur because marriage was not meant to be easy. It was necessary to obey her husband at all costs. Seku treated her like a slave, and now that he was out of work, Fatima had become his only source of income. And because he always needed money to buy alcohol, he would abuse her every time he was in need, and she couldn't provide for him. With four children, she had no choice but to stay and accept her fate.

"You are good for nothing; you are the cause of all my misfortunes. Ever since I married you and brought you here, you have brought me nothing but bad luck. You doomed woman." He said with contempt and rushed to beat her again.

"Please, Seku! Think of our children; I am doing everything I can to make you happy. I gave you all the money I earned yesterday. Today was not busy and I bought groceries with what I had left." She begged him to stop.

"Stop lying to me. It is not because of the groceries. It is because you sent most of your money to your greedy mom. But I will teach you how to respect me. I am your husband, and my needs come first..." And he threw a punch that landed straight on Fatima's jaw. The blow was so hard that she could not help screaming and collapsed to the ground. She sobbed unrestrainedly because of the pain and humiliation.

At that moment, there was a knock on the door. Seku glanced furiously at it and pretended not to hear. Fatima looked terrified. But they knocked louder and louder. He went to look through the peephole and saw two men in uniforms. He returned furiously to her.

"Now, you call the police on me!" He scowled at her.

"I swear to you that I did not call the police. She said, imploring him on her knees, her arms pitifully outstretched towards her husband. "I swear, I did not call anyone."

"We will have a talk about this. Between you, me, and God in this apartment, you will tell me the truth. I knew you were capable of betraying me." He growled threateningly.

"No, my dear husband, I would never have done that." She said, trying to muffle her sobs.

"Who then? We will see if you're right. Go to the bathroom fast. I do not want any trouble here." And talking to himself. "This is how women are! Nobody should trust them!"

Fatima rushed miserably to the toilet to hide. Seku struggled to put on a blank face and went to open the door.

"How can I help you!" He snarled at the two officers.

"Hello, sir. We have been called to this address for domestic problems." One of the officers said.

"I am sorry, but you have got the wrong address," Seku said, trying to dismiss them,

"Really? Are you sure everything is okay?" The officers were doubtful.

"I am quite sure, sir. Everything is fine." He grinned awkwardly.

The two officers looked at him suspiciously, as he was still reeking of alcohol, and his actions lacked coordination. They glanced again at the address they had been given.

"Can we come in, sir, for a minute?" They asked

He hesitated for a moment before letting them pass.

"How many people live here?" They inquired.

"Me, my wife, and my children." Seku unwillingly answered.

"Can we talk to them for a moment?"

"Talk to them for what? I am telling you everything is okay. My wife is having a shower and the kids are already in bed." He was getting annoyed.

The cops looked at each other. This was the address they had been given. They looked around them; one of them went to the bathroom door, listened to the water flow for a moment. He came back to Seku.

"Well, sir, since you say that everything is fine...."

They hesitated again for a moment and decided to head for the exit. They were unaware that two kids, Jalika and her brother Musa, aged nine and seven, were jostling through the darkness of the room to make sure they were missing nothing of what happened. They were peeping through the door lock. Without their parents knowing, they had stolen their mother's phone and decided this time that they were not going to let her get beaten without doing anything. Seeing that the situation was turning to their father's advantage, they opened the door and rushed to the policemen who were about to leave, under the dumbfounded face of Seku. Together they shouted to the police:

"Please, officer... Don't leave. Mum has just been beaten by our father. He told her to hide in the toilet to avoid you..."

And they burst into tears.

CHAPTER
N I N E

The relationship between Christine and Amar became very strained since the last incident. When they separated, they were both confused and lost, not understanding why they had found themselves in such an intricate situation. For Amar, embarrassment and humiliation had given way to a rage that he was trying to suffocate. He did not want to blame everything on Christine. He was aware of the different cultural backgrounds and the hardships she went through. But for some reason, his anger always came back stronger, and he had to face the blunt fact: a denial is a denial. For him, the greatest honor a man could do to a woman was to ask for her hand. And he could not wrap his head around Christine's refusal to get engaged or married. He could only find two reasons for that: either she did not love him enough or trust him enough or both.

Love takes its strength from trust, and if she refused to share her life with him, that was a big red flag for him. Dark ideas started to circulate in his mind. Maybe all she wanted was to use him just to fill her solitude and get rid of him when she saw a man she really loved. Suddenly, the idea came to him that they were different. Maybe she did not want to show up with him in the open. He was only good to sneak into the dark after work, slip into her house when the streets were empty and sneak out before daylight. Was he being rejected a second time? This time not because of his ethnic group but because of the color of his skin. He knew that an interracial relationship was not a simple issue, but he immediately rejected that hypothesis. Christine had the opportunity to reject him from the beginning, and she chose not to. Then what was the real issue? He felt like screaming, punching something, or breaking all the plates around him, something that had never happened to him before.

He took a deep breath to keep his composure and focus on the plates he was pushing furiously through the machine. Christine was suddenly nowhere to be seen and was trying to avoid him. It seemed that she had the ability to read his thoughts from a distance and that she was trying to avoid confrontation. He had never disrespected a woman, but who knew what he would do when she showed up in front of him, and he was not able to contain his anger.

For consolation, he started considering the idea that Christine did not deserve him. She just deserved the kind of men who mistreat women. She had what she deserved in the past because she is incapable of loving men who know how to value women. He did not need that kind of woman in his life either. So, they were even. She was not worth wasting his time anymore, and as far as he was concerned, she no longer existed. Maybe Demba was right.

It was time for him to look for a girl from his culture because he could not continue to live a life of celibacy.

He felt somebody was standing behind him, and he abruptly turned around. It was Christine. He was caught off guard and did not really know what to say. He wanted to yell his frustration at her. If love exists between a man and a woman, could there be no better gift than to propose or marry? He tried to understand, but he could not.

"Are you mad at me?" Christine asked.

"I am not." He growled. He tried to look indifferent, but it did not work. He could not hide the disappointment on his face. He let the flat rack fall on the floor and tiredly stared at her.

"How am I supposed to feel? Be happy about what happened?" He reproachingly said.

"I am just asking you to take it easy. Maybe one day..."

"Maybe one day or maybe never." Amar shrugged his shoulders. "You see. I feel like I am trapped between the devil and the deep blue sea. I love you, but I also think I should do things the right way."

"That's how you feel about our relationship?" She said, surprised. "I love you, and there is nothing wrong with being together. Let's not overreact and take the time to..."

"You think I am overreacting!" He cut her off, and for the first time, he was yelling at her.

The tension was about to get high when a server peeped at dish land and said:

"Christine, you have a table."

She came back a little later and whispered to him in a soft and beseeching voice

"Amar, honey, what do you do with happiness in all this? You always talk about marriage and sacred duty. I think the purpose of everything is the search for happiness, whether through faith or something else. I am not a religious person, but I believe in happiness. You are a believer, and you believe in the same happiness I believe in. Let us live what we have in common and leave our personal beliefs out of this. I am here for you, but you will have to know what you want..." She said in a firm voice.

In the meantime, he had calmed down, but he felt confused. For a moment, he forgot about his convictions, and he no longer knew what he believed in or what he did not believe in. Christine's words rang in his ears as a newfound truth. 'The purpose of everything is the search for happiness', and he could not deny that fact. Right now, with Christine, 'Happiness' was winking at him. And that was hard to reject. He was holding 'Happiness' in his hand. Either he had to seize it or let it go. And once he let it go, he was not sure if he would ever catch it again. Did it make sense to go against one's own happiness? If so, in the name of what? Shouldn't he just go for it as Abdu or Gora had suggested?

They were all gathered in the living room, which happened once in a blue moon.

"Alima's mother passed away yesterday," Demba announced.

"How sad it is for this brave woman. She had just lost her father at the same time last year," said Amar, who did not know her too well, but who remembered the incident.

"Having both parents pass away without having the opportunity to attend their funeral... Life can be so cruel." Demba agreed.

"Life has always been cruel. And the American system only adds to the cruelty of life. There had to be special permits to allow undocumented immigrants to attend the last moments of their loved ones." Gora said.

"You mean making the system humane. We must not forget that it is done deliberately: to make the system so inhumane that it will discourage the unfortunate immigrants and turn their life into hell." Amar said.

"Leaving one's country because of misery and living in greater misery in the host country: fear, loneliness, and homesickness. Life is not fair, but we have to accept our fate." Demba added.

"And worse. You get rejected from both sides of the aisle." Gora added.

He was beginning to get agitated, his mood had completely changed, and he had become the angry man he used to be. His powerful voice was making a desperate plea.

"Here, we are seen only as numbers, figures that increase the rate of unemployment and misery. In Africa, we have become symbols associated with Western Union or MoneyGram. They only remember us when they need help. We only exist if we send money. And when we make the difficult decision to go home or when they deport us, we become outcasts because when we return to our home country, we are often broke... Instead of saving, we send money constantly, two things that rarely go together. And when you go home broke, you sign your own death sentence. You become useless, trashed by your own family. Here we are rejected because the low educated people look at us like we are their enemies, thinking that we come to steal their jobs and make wages lower, and those who employ us, especially the white republican folks, just want to keep us as work slaves. They just want to keep us undocumented to keep the wages low. The irony is that without us, the economy will collapse because there will not be enough hands to do the jobs most US citizens look down at. We are the ones who work mostly in the restaurants, on the farms. We clean buildings, take care of elderly people, make sure the roads are repaired, the lawns are taken care of. Who can imagine eating in a restaurant if there is nobody to wash dishes? You may have the best chefs in the world; if there is no one to clean the dishes, the restaurant will close. And nobody cares about our fate; politicians just use us as pawns as if they were playing chess or checkers."

Amar watched Gora and the words of anger spurting from his mouth, and he knew it was one of those moments when it was not a good idea to interrupt or argue with him. He was ranting against an invisible enemy, and there was no good trying to bring him back to reality. In fact, everything he said made sense, and he was just expressing what they already knew.

Gora suddenly stopped talking, and they were all pondering on what he had just said. Amar could see the rage boiling in his friend and understood that such fierce ideas, combined with a bold personality, made Gora an aggressive man who sometimes wanted to punch people just to silence the anger that was eating him away. Sweat was dripping on his friend's forehead.

Amar thought it was good to appease his friend because they all held out hope that things would change:

"You are absolutely right, my friend. We can only hope that with this new president, things will change."

They were silent for a moment because everyone seemed lost in their own thoughts.

Demba said a few minutes later:

"Tomorrow, I will go and offer my condolences to Alima."

He clearly wanted to talk about something else because he did not want to get bogged down in a debate that was not going to get them anywhere. He had a practical mind, and for him, the time spent on fruitless debates could always be spent otherwise. On the other hand, he did not like that belligerent look in Gora's eyes.

"Poor woman! Her husband was deported a few years ago, and she has to take care of their two children." Demba said.

Gora shook his head sadly. He opened his mouth and was about to say something. But he changed his mind and kept silent.

"We can do it together. What time tomorrow?" Amar suggested, addressing Demba.

"Whatever time suits you. I am on my own schedule." Demba said.

"Well. Can we do it the day after tomorrow, then? Tomorrow I have a very busy day." Amar asked.

"No problem," Demba concluded.

Amar barely knew the lady, but he thought it would be a good thing from time to time to go and sympathize with the misfortune of others. He knew that without Demba, he would never have gone by himself. The latter was like a bridge between them and others because he knew almost everyone. Nobody could say the same about him and Gora.

———

Amar went with Demba and Gora to offer their condolences to Alima. They found her giving instructions to the braiders about a client whose hair was too short but who insisted on braiding it. Alima received them and asked them to sit on one of the sofas in the waiting area. It was a spacious and well-lit salon. Ten braiders were working in pairs on five customers' heads. And their deft fingers were knotting and intertwining the hair of different colors and textures with incredible talent and speed. African American women loved the Senegalese twist and other braid styles of African origins.

Alima had received people for condolences at her house the previous day but had returned to the hair shop because bills and other expenses had to be taken care of, in addition to sending money to Africa. It was a hair salon located on the west side of 7 Mile Road, opposite a gas station, the outside of which customers and hustlers rubbed shoulders all day long. Just a few weeks before, two rival gangs fought, and a stray bullet flew through the salon filled with people. The bullet flew past the petrified women and hit the bathroom wall. In its deadly trajectory, it made a hole through the hair cream pot on the counter, just a few inches from a braider head, who was just leaning on the counter. Everyone had dived on the floor for their lives and remained there for a few minutes, too terrified to budge. Death had been so close. They could hear the bullets being exchanged in the street for a few seconds before some of the assailants fled in a getaway car, leaving one person dead and another seriously injured. And it was a miracle that the bullet did not hit anyone in the salon because there were at least a dozen people. The braiders often remembered that incident when they talked about the ephemeral aspect of life, especially in a country like America, mainly in a city like Detroit or Chicago, where the gift of life could be taken away at any time. You can be alive one minute and be dead the next because of a bullet meant for somebody else.

"We have learned the sad news, and we are here to offer our condolences. This is Gora and Amar; they are my roommates. I do not think you meet often." Demba introduced his two friends.

Alima looked at them and searched in her memory, but she did not seem to remember their faces.

"We might have met in some of our community get-togethers, and maybe we did not have the opportunity to be introduced. You know, I am always at the hair salon and, you are certainly busy with your jobs as well." She said.

"I have to admit I don't usually go to those meetings. I like to stay home when I do not go to work." Amar replied.

"I have already seen your face somewhere. I think I have seen you at the 'Marabout House'. But I did not know your name." Gora added after peering at her.

"You're right. I am regularly at the Marabout House. I go there almost every Monday night..." Alima said.

The Marabout House was a building bought by the Senegalese community to host religious events and have gatherings for everything related to the community. It is also the Islamic center and consists of a mosque, a conference room, and classrooms for religious studies. The 'Marabout' is the spiritual guide of a part of the Senegalese community hence the name of the center. He would visit his disciples once or twice a year.

"I do not need to introduce myself; everyone knows me because I go everywhere," Demba said, with a grin on his face. He immediately pulled himself together, realizing the solemnity of the moment.

"We are especially fortunate to have you here, Demba. I cannot thank you enough for everything you do for me and my braiders, and everybody says the same good thing about you. Day and night, you make sure our sisters get to their workplaces or homes safely at a fair price. You can be reached at any time of night or day, and you are always nice to everybody."

She was making inferences to the other African drivers who were far from being as kind as Demba. He had compassion and patience, something most drivers lacked. Most of them only took the call of the braiders when business was slow and often spent their time quarreling with them. Sometimes it was a well-deserved fight because some braiders, even though they make good money, not only hardly ever gave tips, but also were always trying to bargain to avoid paying a normal fare.

"It is my duty to look after you and take care of you. You are our sisters and our wives, and on my side, I will do everything I can to help. We want to tell you to keep being strong like you always have been. You have gone through a lot, but you are always the same strong woman. We face all this terrible punishment that prevents us from going home to attend to our sick parents, to say goodbye to them in their last moment and even to attend their funeral. No punishment is more painful than that, but when you do not have a choice, you just suffer in silence. We cannot remedy this suffering or put an end to it, but we are with you with all our hearts in these difficult moments." Demba said.

One of the braiders approached, she greeted them and said:

"Sorry to bother you, gentlemen, but Alima, I think you are going to have to talk to the customer. She does not know what she wants. She wants us to take down what we already braided because she is not sure she will like the style."

"That's not going to happen. Does she think we do not have anything else to do? Excuse me, guys, I will be right back." She got up, and her big ample dress made a swishing noise.

The braider did not look at them when she was talking to Alima, but something in her voice and her appearance made Amar startle. He was sure he had met that woman somewhere in the past. Was it possible that it was her?

"Aisha?" He said, not aware that he was thinking aloud.

The lady turned around, and the surprise made her drop the hair scissors she had in her hand... Aisha had just recognized Amar, and both remained speechless.

"It looks like you two know each other," Demba said, intrigued by the look in their eyes.

"That's right... We have met... years ago." Aisha said, still in shock.

Amar got up instantly and walked to Aisha. They stood before each other, not sure what to do. They hesitated before falling into each other's arms. They hugged in silence. Aisha detached herself slowly, and Amar said:

"What a small world! I had never imagined that we would meet again one day. How are you, Aisha?"

"I'm doing well. Amar. What a surprise?"

"You have not changed a lot, Aisha."

"You haven't either." She replied in a simple tone.

People were watching the sudden encounter and realized that these two people had once shared some bond, and the intensity in the air indicated that the past had gently sneaked through the door and was watching from a corner of the shop, like an invisible accomplice.

"I did not know you were here. How long have you been in this country?" Amar asked.

"It's been a few years now. I heard you left some years earlier, but I didn't know what state you were in... and you never said 'Goodbye'." She tried to smile but her eyes were sad. A heavy silence fell between them. They felt a little uncomfortable with all those eyes on them. After the surprise, old emotions started ramping up, and Amar felt he had to say something, but only something that could be told between the two of them, far from the curious eyes.

"Let me take your phone number and we will talk." Amar requested.

They exchanged their numbers, and Aisha went back to work. Amar sighed and regained his seat while Gora, who could not wait, was already murmuring in his friend's ears. But Amar could not focus on what Gora was saying. His eyes were glued on Aisha. She had gained a little weight but had kept the same beauty, the same serious and profound look, which awakened in him so many memories.

PART

TWO

CHAPTER
TEN

As usual, Fatima had returned late from the hair salon and was busy in the kitchen. But now she was no longer worried about being abused. She had not felt that relieved for a long time and was even humming some old song from her village. Some song long forgotten that had been revived because of her newfound happiness. She owed her freedom to her children, who had taken their courage with both hands and secretly warned the police. Since that famous night, things had changed for the better. Her refusal to press charges had saved Seku from jail, but he had been aware of the imminent danger he had exposed himself to. Most importantly, he had realized the damages he had been inflicting on his family and the resentment and hatred that had grown into his kids' hearts. He had decided to repent and be as good as he could be.

That night, he was taken to the police station by the two officers, and the balance of power had suddenly shifted. His fate was in the hands of Fatima and the kids, and he had to beg his wife to forgive him. He swore that he was going to change and that he had been a man possessed by the devil, and the first thing he needed was prayers to get rid of the demons that turned him against his wife and children.

He kept his promise as soon as he was released because he knew he could be deported if he returned to the police for domestic violence. He went to the mosque and asked for prayers for himself and his family. He found a job and stopped drinking. He had become very gentle to his wife and children. The atmosphere of the apartment had become that of a normal family, and now Jalika, the eldest daughter, was proudly helping her mom in the kitchen while Musa played in the living room with the little ones. Seku had finally found a night job in one of the factories in the suburb, and during the day, after having some rest, he would take care of the kids while Fatima was at work.

Fatima thought of everything she had endured, and all of a sudden how God had arranged things thanks to her little guardian angels. She stopped in the middle of the kitchen and looked dreamily at the older girl who was washing the dishes. Jalika felt her mother's gaze on her and turned around to face her. Her mother was pretty, and she was even more beautiful with those lovely dimples on her cheek when she smiled. She felt so proud of being able to revive that rare smile, which had almost died forever, crushed by grief and sorrow. She loved the joy that irradiated her mom's refined face ornated with beautiful almond eyes. Timidly, she smiled at her and asked:

"What, Mommy?"

"Come here, my love."

110

She went to snuggle up to her mother, and in silence, they felt the fullness of that moment. Fatima clutched her child to her heart, experiencing a happiness she had never experienced before. With her eyes closed, she could think of only one thing: "Thank you, Lord! Thank you, Lord!"

She loved all her kids, but she loved her daughter more than anything else. She was almost ten, and the first signs of puberty were precociously appearing in her fragile body. She could not help thinking about herself when she was the same age. That atrocious day always came to her mind when she had been woken up in the middle of the night and taken somewhere in the wood with a group of other girls. All of them had been blindfolded and had been forced to dance in a circle surrounded by the songs and claps of older women. She was terrified and could feel the terror of the other girls. After being exhausted by several dances, they were given that very sour and oily beverage they had to drink while their clothes were being taken off. She could feel callous hands rub her whole naked body with the same mysterious beverage she had been asked to drink. Minutes later, they were asked by the clueless voice of an old woman to line up in front of some place that felt like a big hut. One by one, they would be taken inside the hut, and while the older women outside would try to cover up with songs and hand-clapping, the painful shriek of young girls being deprived of a part of their 'womanhood' with a piece of dirty blade would pierce the somber night. It was fueled by the sordid idea of turning off any premature 'sexual desire' in girls and keeping them virgins until they married. Fatima clasped her daughter even more. She would never allow her to go to her village until she became a fully grown-up woman.

She went through a lot in the US, but she was happy to be here. At least what happened to her in her native country would never happen to her daughters. They would never be excised or subject to forced marriage as long as they lived in this country. She loved the US because they respected women's rights. Her abusive husband would never have been worried if they lived in Africa. So many women were suffering in silence, and she wished more was done in her native country to protect them. In the US, a spouse would have to abide by the law if he did not want trouble. Apparently, Seku had learned his lesson, and she was thankful to her courageous and smart kids.

Amar and his two roommates took turns cooking in the apartment once a week to save on food. This at least ensured them something to eat for the week. It was Amar's turn to prepare the meal. He went to the local supermarket to do his shopping. Nearby, the police were talking to a group of kids, who appeared to have fought between themselves outside the supermarket. Funny country where the police were called for twelve-year-old kids who fought between them, a problem easily solved by any adult in Africa. Here, they had to call the police and sometimes it might escalate into tragedy, especially when the young people are black. Amar quickly entered the supermarket and headed to the grocery shelves. He picked some vegetables, oil, and some fruits. He also grabbed a bag of rice. Almost all the food they prepared included rice. He needed some tropical vegetables such as cassava and okra, but they could only be found in African stores. Luckily, there was one not far from the apartment.

He turned on the stove and put some oil in the pot. He avoided putting too much oil and salt in his meals. African women love greasy, spicy, and salty foods and it is not very healthy. He thought of the irony of his situation. If he were in Africa, women would have made fun of him, because cooking was not for men. Women take care of cooking and cleaning. The stories of men who cook, wash dishes and clean houses bring laughter and astonishment for people who never traveled out of Africa. But those same people love the money sent by the people they make fun of because money has no smell.

He considered the pile of vegetables and fruit he had bought from the grocery store for a few bucks. As far as food is concerned, life in America is good. The supermarkets are full of food, and if you work hard, you will never starve. He had been hungry for much of his life and had learned to respect food and to thank the lord whenever he had the privilege to feed himself decently. Unfortunately, for many families in Africa, decent food was never to be taken for granted, and sometimes even working hard does not guarantee food on the table.

He remembered the hard times spent at the university without a scholarship and without close relatives to help him pay for food or room. He would spend the night with roommates who were in the same condition as him, in a small stifling room located in the Campus that they had named 'Room Zero'. They called it room zero because there was no number at the door. It was a mop room and was used by the campus janitors to keep their cleaning equipment. It was at the end of the hall, and one of their classmates, whose uncle was a janitor, had been able to get them to sleep there. They would pile up in the tiny space to share food and shelter. Five of them would spend the night there, and during the day, five others would join to share the food they managed to get from the restaurant. The small group had developed a restaurant ticket management system to allow everyone to put some food in their mouth.

They usually got one week-worth supply of tickets every month from the government, and they put all the tickets together and at lunch or dinner time they only used three tickets for the whole group. They would take one big bowl to the campus restaurant and have the servers put a big portion of food that they would take to Room Zero and share. By doing so, they could make the tickets go further. Servants and cooks understood their situation and would cooperate just to help them feed themselves.

When the supply ran out, those who could afford it would pitch in more tickets so the whole group could be fed. He was one of those who could not afford to bring in more tickets and had to suffer the contemptuous gaze of some of his roommates. He would get up after just two or three spoonfuls because he rarely had money to help buy a meal ticket.

When he stayed several days without being able to contribute a ticket, he would go for a walk at dinner time. He couldn't do that during lunch because he needed to eat to keep a bit of energy to attend classes, but in the evening, he would skip dinner so as not to suffer the feeling of being considered a 'parasite'.

One night, during one of his solitary walks, he found out that place where some homeless people would meet around dusk in a dumpster of the Teacher's School restaurant where leftovers were put in clean plastic bags and deposited in the trash. There would be a small line of homeless and poor people, and one of them would serve the food in empty tomato cans, plastic, or paper wraps. He would stand in line and get his share of food. That place became his refuge, and he would go there two or three times a week so as not to starve.

There was that night he had decided not to go, but he got so hungry that he could not keep his promise. By the time he had arrived, it was too late, and the only creature he found was a cat with its head plunged into one tomato can. He rushed to the cat and kicked it away. He realized that the pot was empty and that the poor cat was just another starving soul like him. Furious, he turned back, walking as fast as he could until exhausted by his effort, he sat at the side of the road on a public bench. He thought of the cat and tried to make fun of himself, thinking that laughing it off could appease his hunger. He burst out laughing, but it was not funny. He suddenly broke down and took his head in his hands. Big tears dripped down his bony cheeks, eroded by hunger and lack of sleep. He curled up on the bench like a dark lump of rags by the dimly lit road, his head between his knees, wondering what had become of his dream and his life. It had come down to fighting with a hungry cat for food leftovers.

Since that night, he did not have the courage to return to the place. He chose to confront the scornful gaze from some and the compassionate smiles from others. Some people were generous by nature and were happy to share the little they had with people who had nothing. Others were selfish and mean, and they hated to share. But besides the bitter memories, he could also remember the joy and enthusiasm of being young and innocent, able to absorb and enjoy any little pleasure life could offer. There were those great moments of togetherness when huddled against each other over a cup of tea, they mulled over the reflections of Suley the Philosopher or when they laughed at the jokes of Badu the Comedian.

"You see," said Suley the Philosopher, "Everything is relative in life, even age. You think the first-born is the older. You are certainly wrong because the older is not the one who was born first but the one who dies first. One can be older than his father, older than his old brother, older than his friend of the same age... I know it's hard for ordinary heads like you to understand. But see? My younger brother died five years ago. However, it is said that eternal life begins after death. So, he will have started his eternal life before me and when I die, he will be my big brother because the law of relativity applies in the afterlife: one cannot be older here and there at the same time. So, technically, he will be older than me there since he will have resurrected first. And as life on earth is only the mirage of that of the afterlife... His longevity will last more than mine."

"You're assuming that he'll resurrect first, but we've learned that everyone will resurrect at the same time, so your theory turns out to be wrong." Assan interrupted him.

"If what you say is true, then we must admit that injustice will never end in this world because we inherit it from God. The dead and the living are not treated the same way. How can we have the privilege of being born first and not resurrect first when we die first?"

"Because life is a privilege, not death.... In any case, I have no desire to resurrect first. Imagine having in front of you a host of estranged ancestors you had never met before and the anxiety of waiting for the people you used to be close to on earth. I'd rather wait and be surrounded by my immediate family and friends." Musa said.

He would rarely take part in those debates and contented himself to listen to the Philosopher who would stubbornly try to convince everybody else that he was right. Suley would go on in his assertion without really listening to others, pleased to have created the controversy.

And often Badu the comedian had to interrupt the debate by kicking off with one of his funny stories.

"We hear you Suley. We all know you like to talk about serious matters like death and find answers to issues that are older than your great-grandparents. I worry that one day this poor brain of yours is going to blow up because you are demanding too much from it. Now, let's move on to non-serious matters, guys, we need some laughter here. Let me tell you about that Serer guy who was invited by his best friend's girlfriend. This guy, like every good Serer, could not tell the difference between coffee and Coca-Cola. When he went with his friend to visit the girlfriend's house, the girl served them some Coca-Cola for refreshment. When the guy grabs his drink and saw that it was cold, he got mad and did not take a single sip. The girl, having noticed the guy's grumpy face, asked him:

"What's going on, honey? Is there something wrong?"

And the guy responded visibly furious:

"I was told that the girls of the city did not know how to treat people, and I just have the evidence of it. In my village, when someone serves you coffee, first it's always hot, then there's always a piece of bread or crackers to go

117

with it. You city girls are so weird!"

The girl, shaken with laughter, thought the guy was messing with her, she managed to say:

"You really like coffee. I absolutely have to go and prepare some for you."

And the guy, looking very serious, replied:

"You can't even realize how much I love coffee. If the ocean was made of coffee... I would only hang out by the beach and the fish would be my best friends."

Everyone burst out laughing, and it was the beginning of another series of talks where everyone would try to tell a funny story...

"The story I have for you today is about that lady who was looking for a job," Amidu said. "She said to the other girls waiting for an interview. 'I need that job, and I am going to do everything that it takes to get it.' She did not realize the hiring manager overheard her. When it was her turn, and she went to the interview office. The man asked her: 'Are you willing to do anything to get this job?' She said: 'Anything', and she started to unbutton her shirt. The man asked again: 'Are you sure?' The lady said: 'Anything' and she took off her shirt. 'Anything?' 'Anything', and she took off her bra. 'Anything?' 'Anything', and she took off everything. When she was completely naked, the man took the clothes and told the lady. 'Good. Now go outside and walk down the street for five minutes. When you come back, the job is yours'. The lady fainted...

"And what about the three guys from the psychiatric center who wanted to escape. They met in secret and had a plan of escape. So one of them said: 'Here is our plan. We have to be smart and do it one by one so as not to draw anybody's attention. One of us would go first. If the gate is open and the security guard is sitting by the left side of the gate, you will go right and tiptoe your way out; if the guard is sitting by the right side, go left.' They all agreed that was a good plan. So, the first guy went and came back a few minutes later. 'Guys, there is a problem. The gate is wide open but there is no security guard.' They were all disappointed and said: 'Our plan has failed. Let's try again tomorrow'!"

It helped them to pass a good moment and fight the stress and anxiety that resulted from the dark prospect of the future. College had become just a place where it was necessary to take refuge and spend time away because after that there was nothing else to do. With or without a college degree, the same fate was waiting for most of the students. Unemployment and idleness. Therefore, most would rather stay within the College campus and retake classes than graduate earlier just to avoid the contemptuous eyes of society.

Parents and relatives were expecting a payback of all the money they invested on them. But with no employment in view and no bright prospect, they would keep huddling in Room Zero, sharing the funny, the sad and the unfortunate fate that brought them together. At home, isolation, loneliness, and depression would be their daily companion.

Now, he couldn't help smiling when thinking about that period of his life, which was wrapped up in the tender webs of nostalgia. He checked the boiling pot and started to throw in the vegetable he had neatly peeled.

Despite his courage and motivation, he was not able to pass the second year of university and had returned to his hometown with a bitter heart and empty hands. And every morning he went to the door of the house, disoriented and jobless like so many others who get out of college. He would just stand outside the house or roam in the neighborhood, watching people commuting to their daily activities. Long lines of students leaving for school, workers heading to their shops and housewives, modestly dressed and their scarves perfectly poised on their heads, walking gracefully and nonchalantly to the market. Late sellers and traders hurrying past not to miss the first transactions of the day.

He liked to watch the students advance in groups or alone towards the same places, the same objectives, and different dreams. Apart from wandering in the neighborhood or in the woods, he had known no other destination than school. Summer vacations spent with distant relatives were unknown to him. The first day he had traveled was when he went to college in the capital. The school was the place from which his dream was born, had grown up and over the years had finally scattered like dead leaves through the dry wind of the Sahel, that place on the planet where dreams, like plants, men, and animals, had short life expectancies. No matter how he hung on to his dream of success, the harsh and sterile reality had crushed it, like that shrub there, dying under a blazing sun in a cloudless sky...

But sometimes, good things happen after bad things. From the setback and the deep humiliation he had from his short relationship with Aisha, he decided it was time for him to leave his small town permanently and fight for survival in the capital. He went to rejoin his friends in room zero for a place to sleep and took up any small job he could to survive. He was also able to join a youth club that had some connection with YMCA in the US. And by chance, he got selected for a summer camp vacation for six weeks. When the camp ended, he decided, like others had advised him, to overstay his exchange student visa. What was the point of returning if nothing important was waiting for him?

There was not even a room anymore to accommodate him in his family of adoption. Without employment to fly on their own, most young adults had to share the meager pensions of parents and grandparents, contenting themselves with the leftovers of life while helplessly witnessing the looting of the country's wealth by the corrupt people in power. The politicians, without any remorse and scruples, celebrated in broad daylight, spent and spoiled money extravagantly, self-consciously crushing the dreams and hopes of present and future generations.

CHAPTER
ELEVEN

Amar entered the large complex that was located at 8 Mile and Lahser Road. He dialed the room number and waited a few seconds before the entrance door clicked open and gave access to the building. He went to the second floor and knocked at an apartment that opened, and Aisha stepped aside to let him pass before locking back the door. She told him in a weary voice to take a seat in one of the black leather couches in the living room. It was a two-bedroom apartment. The living room was quiet and discreetly furnished. The TV was already off, and Aisha looked tired and sleepy.

There was an awkward silence as she sat in the opposite chair, facing him. She stared at him questioningly and seemed ready to listen to what he was about to say. After their unexpected encounter, Amar asked to talk to her the same day after work. Aisha did not seem very willing to talk to him, but he had insisted so much that she had decided to give him her address. He had wanted them to meet somewhere over a small meal, but Aisha almost never went out. Her life revolved around the hair salon and her apartment.

Aisha explained to him how her life had never been the same since that incident. She had kept wishing that they could find a way to see each other and how big her disappointment was when she learned that he left for the capital. Amar also learned that Aisha's uncle passed away a couple of years ago.

"Aisha, I know you could be mad at me for disappearing. But what could I do? And I did not have anything to offer you except my heart. No job, no future, no hope. All I could bring you was despair and unhappiness because your family would not support that relationship. It was better that way. I didn't have anything to lose, but you were a good woman from a 'good' family; you had everything to lose. I did not want to put you in trouble with your family." He regretfully explained.

"I tried to understand, Amar, but it was hard. Sometimes, happiness has a price. I was ready to fight for you, but you didn't give me that chance. You have to stand for what you believe, and our generation should not let themselves be intimidated or forced into something that does not reflect our world. We cannot live in our ancestors' time." Aisha said sadly.

"I agree with you. But there was just too much failure going on in my life, and I still believe it would have been unfair of me to drag you into that. I would not forgive myself for putting you in a bad relationship with your family, knowing I had nothing to offer you. I had too much love and respect for you."

"Respect, maybe. But love! Maybe you did not love me

enough..."

Her voice sounded neutral, but Amar could still catch the profound reproach that had not faded through the years.

"I swear I could not take you off my head. I ..." He suddenly realized the awkwardness of the situation. They had not seen each other for more than eight years, and a lot of things may have happened.

"By the way... what has your life become?" He asked.

"I got into an arranged marriage with a cousin, and we both found out it was a mistake. Neither of us was happy. There was no love between us, and besides, I couldn't give him a child after four years. So, of course, the marriage ended, and I had an opportunity to travel, and I seized it." She tried to smile. "I traveled and left the past behind me, like you."

"And here we are, brought back in the same past," Amar said with some nostalgia in his voice. I kept your letter with me. It was beautiful... and sorry for not showing any sign of life.

Aisha's face lit up a little bit.

"Oh... that letter? I am sure you got rid of it."

"I did... just because it made me suffer more. But I used to sleep with it... Aisha, did you really feel something for me?"

"Feel! You were my world, and I was obsessed with you! What's the point now, Amar? Don't tell me you are still single."

"I still am, Aisha..."

The silence that followed was more eloquent than words. In the midst of the silence, the past had arisen like a colorful ghost, turning the apartment into scenes where nostalgia, regret and bitterness mingled in a symphony of a thousand sighs; memories danced in the air, bringing with them a sense of lost youth.

The unexpected encounter with Aisha had changed Amar's prospects. He had started to enjoy his life with Christine again, encouraged by Gora's words. If Gora could go out with different women and feel good about it, why not him! He could not help asking himself whether God had made all men with the same materials. Why do some people feel more remorseful than others? He liked Christine's company and felt happy with her, but their relationship lacked the tranquility of the soul that the seal of marriage guaranteed. Sometimes he was haunted in his sleep and would wake up in the middle of the night sweating and shivering, chased by demons who accused him of having deviated from his path. He started to live with the feeling that something terrible was going to happen to him. He then realized that his happiness with Christine lacked the spiritual foundation he needed. A stable happiness anchored in solid spiritual bases provides tranquility of mind and fullness of life. Aisha had reappeared at that moment in his life where he was in dire need of solace, and he was tempted to see this as a sign of fate that wanted to give him a second chance to repent and find the right way.

Every morning Gora commuted to his place of work, located in the suburbs of Detroit. He had been working for a long time in this auto parts factory, and his ears were used to the deafening noises of robot machines that filled

the place. Huge steel hands were cutting, shaping, polish-
ing, and conveying at a frantic pace. Workers were adjust-
ing, evaluating, controlling, watching without flinching. It
was necessary to be on the lookout for the slightest false
note, the slightest error or malfunction of the machines
that were running in a large circular movement where
each piece represented a puzzle of the finished product.

The workers had to be very alert because the parts
were produced in an accelerated and monotonous rhythm,
and they had to quickly inspect them, stick labels, and put
the parts with defects in a large metal container. The noise
was surreal, but he was used to it. He was a component of
the machines and had to keep up with their frenzied pace.
If he were a little behind, he would block the entire chain
process, and the siren would go off and alert the
managers. They would rush to see what was going on, and
they had to be given a good reason. Fatigue was not one of
them. Either you were able to keep up with the machine,
or you were replaced like one of the broken parts.

There was a production to be made, a result to be
reached, a performance to be achieved every day of every
week. It was the tyranny of numbers, and it was all about
production. It was necessary to deliver the orders on time
and maintain a good level of performance to avoid losing
one's place in the market. Sometimes production is ahead
because the machines had been efficient, without mechan-
ical stops or serious failure. In this case, there were quite
a few technical stops, and it was an opportunity to clean
up the area. He was given a certain perimeter that he had
to keep clean in downtime moments. He had to go to one
of the areas where the floor was usually flooded with
chemical waste. It was all sticky, and a large amount of

strong detergent had to be used to clean it up.

He did not know the nature of the product that he was using for cleaning, but the strong and stifling smell made him think it must be a dangerous product. In fact, it must have been the cause of the pain he often felt in his chest. Sometimes the pain was acute and prevented him from sleeping or breathing well. He had also developed dark rashes on the skin. The itching was sometimes so strong that he was forced to massage his body with ointment bought at the pharmacy. For the lung, he was afraid to go to the doctor. He was afraid that the latter would reveal to him some serious illness that would prevent him from working. He did not trust these doctors, who were always very prompt to conclude serious diagnoses. And even if that were the case and he decided to hide it from his employers, he was afraid the doctor could call them to reveal his condition. He was afraid of the consequences because he had no right to get sick. He had come to work and send money but not to fall sick and be prevented from working. He would rather be dead and gone than be helpless and homeless, not being able to take care of himself and others. The alarm called for a lunch break, and he headed to the cafeteria to warm up the lunch he had brought with him.

Gora was thinking of his friend Amar. He liked Amar because he was everything he wanted to be. He was calm, moderate, simple, honest, and respectful. He might be angry at the whole world, but he never could feel anger for him and had always considered him as his own brother. He knew he was a difficult person to live with, but Amar understood him and had always supported and listened to him. It was Amar who had brought him into the apartment because he had never been able to get along well with others. Apart from his one confrontation with Demba, there had never been any issue because Amar had tried to make him a better person. He had taught him to pray and to have faith in God. He understood that his relationship with Christine was not simple for him because he was a devout person, but he wished he could follow his advice for his own personal well-being. A life without a woman was a monotonous and useless life.

What worried him now was Aisha showing up into the picture. Amar was on the verge of regaining a touch of happiness because until now, he had lived a dull life, and part of him was still drenched in the past. He had begun to see in his face a new glow that he had never seen before. He was happy for him even if sometimes a glimmer of fear would appear in his friend's eyes like a child who had been caught in some guilty act. The reality was that he was a pure-hearted, innocent person, and guilt resonated more heavily on his soul than others. His past resurfaced out of nowhere and seemed ready to take over the present. He feared that Amar's fragile heart and soul were not equipped to support that kind of challenge.

Both Aisha and Christine seemed to be respectable women. Both could have been a good choice for him. But life was not so simple, and in love, there was no mercy. Hearts, like wild animals, trample and tear each other apart to triumph. Only the best is not always the one who wins. Gora shook his head and felt sorry for his friend. He had never had such problems because he had always had many girlfriends. Besides, he avoided women who were looking for serious relationships. He already had a wife waiting for him in his country, with whom he only communicated through the phone and social media. He did not know when he was going to see her again or if he was ever going to see her again. All he knew was that he needed a woman, and as long as he could find one, he would not bother himself with moral principles. But Amar was different, and he did not want him to suffer because of this delicate situation. For once, he felt helpless, and all he could do was pray for him.

In his clear and melodious voice, the cleric or 'Imam' of the mosque recited an unusually long Surat on this morning of the feast of Eid. With striking lyricism, he navigated through the various verses that made up the Surat. The intonations of his voice went up and down, the rhythm accelerated and slowed according to the gravity and meaning of the verse. The softness of the tone reflected the promises of happiness in the luxurious mansions and beautiful meadows of Paradise, and at times, his voice changed to something chilling and sad, foreshadowing the terrible punishments intended for the nonbelievers and infidels.

In the mosque located at Five Mile Road, most members were from West Africa, and they did not speak Arabic. Hardly any of them understood the meaning of the verses, but the air was filled with an intense sense of communion and meditation. Amar was carried away by the sound of the cleric's captivating voice. He liked to sway nonchalantly while waiting for the signal to bow before the Lord, begging for forgiveness and salvation.

After the prayer, the cleric made two long sermons that taught peace, solidarity, and compassion. Then he encouraged each Muslim to ask forgiveness from their neighbors and shake their hands. The believers and their families were invited to come back in the afternoon for the traditional barbecue. The children circulated between the adults and asked for their gift money. Everyone looked happy. It was reminiscent of Africa where all the family members would gather around a big meal, and in the evening, there was a constant movement between members of the community and the extended family where fathers, uncles, grandparents, sisters, aunts, mother, and friends would visit one another; and the children would go from house to house to ask for presents. The community was trying to revive the good warm African atmospheres in this cold environment. A day without work, without stress, without loneliness. A day when they felt like they were back in their home country.

Amar felt invigorated, away from the monotonous life he led inside his little corner as a dishwasher. He enjoyed the air of freedom and celebration and peered at the group of women. He was hoping to catch a glimpse of Aisha. They were all beautiful, wrapped in loose and colorful dresses, and their headscarves reflected a myriad of colors that danced through the shy rays of the sun. They repented for the sins, forgave, and asked for forgiveness from one another, wished one another better health, hugged, and laughed and talked, and the whole thing produced a cocktail of joy and happiness that diluted the sorrows and the fears.

Amar was looking forward to the evening as he was invited by Aisha. He circulated in the crowd and distractedly stretched his hand here and there to people mostly unknown to him, saying greetings and words of peace. Most men wore white 'boubou' with a hat on their heads, while some chose to put more expensive and colorful costumes on. People went to shake hands with the Imam. Amar saw at a distance Abdu surrounded by some of his friends, but he chose not to join them and went on his way. People spoke four or five different languages, representing Africa in its diversity. They immortalized the moment by taking pictures and selfies. He could not see Aisha. Maybe she had come late and withdrawn a little earlier. Anyway, the most important thing was done, and he sneaked out of the mosque. He wanted to get some rest before going to visit her.

Later in the afternoon, he went to find Aisha. When the latter opened the apartment door, he was welcomed by the smell of grilled lamb.

"I hope I am not late."

"You're right on time. Fatu and I had just started setting the table."

Aisha had explained to him on the phone that she and her roommate Fatu were preparing dinner, and the latter had invited her boyfriend too. So they had agreed to have a small dinner together. Amar followed Aisha to the living room, where Fatu was already settled with her boyfriend.

"This is Amar, and this is Fatu and her boyfriend, Khalil."

Smiles and handshakes were exchanged as the two women returned to the kitchen and let the men talk. Khalil had just arrived in the United States a few months ago and was still under the spell of the modern world that offered to his rural eyes so many facilities and beautiful structures.

He was a burly man with a big voice, and he loved to make large gestures when he spoke as if the words were not enough to express his huge enthusiasm. He spoke a lot, and Amar had to instinctively dodge his large hands that came too near to his face.

"What a wonderful country America is." He said in Wolof, one of the most popular languages in Senegal. "I won the green card lottery. I heard that many Africans are here illegally. I wonder what has gotten in those people's minds. If you come here legally, you have so many opportunities. I had no problem finding a job. But I wonder why people are in such a hurry in this country. Everybody walks fast, drives fast, eats fast as if the world is going to end tomorrow. I am struggling with the fast pace of life and with the language, of course. But I am learning English. I love this country because there is a job. And so many supermarkets and restaurants! How long have you been here, brother?"

"Almost ten years." Amar said in an evasive voice, already feeling uncomfortable with the talkative man.

"My God! You have been here for a long time, my brother. I guess you speak good English. I heard some people stay here for twenty years without ever going back to Africa. I could never do that. My parents are old, and I need to visit them. And... lowering his voice, I have a wife and kids there. But I think I might have another wife here too. One there, one here." He winked at him.

"You have a green card. How about bringing your wife here?" Amar asked out of curiosity.

"She is taking care of our kids, man, and she is getting old. I need me a young woman who takes care of myself." He grinned, trying to lower his voice and looking in the direction of the kitchen.

Amar was stunned by the man's selfishness and was not surprised why he did not like him in the first place.

"What about you, my friend? Have you been to Africa recently?"

"No, said Amar feeling embarrassed. Actually, I can't go home because I couldn't come back here anymore if I did. I do not have my green card yet."

"How sad, my brother! You are missing out so much in the country. But don't give up. I even heard that this president is going to legalize undocumented people. Soon you will be able to return to the country. I bet you will be lost when you set foot there. Everything has changed. Our current president is working hard so our country can take off a little."

"Dinner is ready, guys. Everybody! Have a seat at the table!" Fatu called.

Amar was relieved to have a break from Khalil's annoying conversation. Both women were good cooks, and the dinner was delicious. The well-grilled and well-seasoned lamb with onion sauce and fries brought sweet memories of the happy days of Eid in Africa, where each family prepared a big dinner and shared it with the poor and street children. It was one of the few days when everyone ate enough meat. He did not sleep on the street, but he never had enough to eat, except for the day of Eid.

After dinner, they cheered and took pictures and selfies on their phones. It was important to send a picture to the family back home to show that apart from work, there was some life too, in America. Then, Fatu took Khalil to her room while Amar and Aisha stayed in the living room. They were silently staring at the TV, but their minds were elsewhere. Old memories awoke in their minds, and they let themselves get gently lulled by the nostalgic tides of the past. They were trying to remember the short but intense moments they spent together, the long walks, the things they could have done together or the life they would have had together if things went the ways they hoped. But at some point, they had exhausted all the memories, and they were forced to look at each other and face the overwhelming reality that brought them together. After the regrets and bitterness of the past, they found themselves again like two teenagers dazzled by the promises of the heart, a promise that fate had once denied, and which, realizing its blunder had offered them a second chance.

As he held Aisha in his hands, he couldn't help thinking about Christine and wondered how he had gotten himself in this position. He felt like his heart was divided into two parts, and each part was filled with the love of a different woman. He was sure to have some feeling for Christine, but he was not aware that the other part of him was still hanging on to the past. He could not help the overflow of emotion that invaded him when he saw Aisha again. Undoubtedly, he still loved her. He had never anticipated that kind of situation, and he knew the time would come when he would have to choose between the two women. He was not Gora, and he was not programmed to handle more than one woman at a time. He was a bad liar and a bad cheater. He would be caught before he knew it.

Each of the two women embodied for him the promises of a happy and full life. Why was destiny tricking him into choosing between them? He would forcibly have to let one of them down, and he sensed he would not come out of it unscathed. He was not able to enjoy the moment because of the many uncertainties ahead of him. How would Christine react if she knew he had cheated on her? How would Aisha react if she knew he had lied to her about not having a girlfriend? He felt deep anxiety crawling all over him.

Aisha noticed he was suddenly absent-minded

"Are you okay, Amar? I want you to feel at home and enjoy yourself? No thinking about work or anything." She said, resting her head on his shoulder.

"I feel at home. I missed this moment." He patted her hair and tried to live the moment. But back in his head, he could not help thinking about the troubled waters he was wading into.

CHAPTER
TWELVE

Christine was having the worst day of her life. She had come from her doctor's appointment with Josh, and he had disclosed to her the frightening news: Josh had cancer. She had never thought the red spots on his skin and his shortness of breath could be the symptoms of a serious condition. How could such a lovely and young soul be subject to such terrible disease? She always thought cancer was something for the elderly, people at the twilight of their life. That horrible news just shattered her life. How could she face her little baby and tell him he had cancer and that he might not be able to live a normal and long life? She envisioned the future of her son laying down on his bed and being too weak to walk or play, and her heart sank. How could she bear such a sight?

Her whole life was about to change because she might not only have to be a mother but also a caregiver. Now she knew she was right in not saying yes to Amar. She loved him to death, but her son came first. She already knew she could not be the good and perfect wife that Amar wanted, but her son's condition would make matters worse. In the near future, when her son might need to have serious treatments, he might need her whole attention, and it would be almost impossible for her to always take good care of Amar. For now, she did not need Amar to know about it. She did not want anybody to pity her or her son. Josh was a strong and brave little kid, and she was almost certain he would recover from the disease. The doctor told her the cancer was detected at an early stage, and he believed with the right treatment, they might stop the progress. They tried to comfort her, but they could not be a hundred percent sure. With cancer, nobody can ever be sure, even if cured, that it would not come back. Whatever the result, her baby was the last person to deserve that. She pulled in front of the apartment and grabbed a napkin to dry her tears. She was a strong woman, and her son never saw her drop a tear. She needed to keep strong for him.

In the evening, after her night shift she saw Abdu approaching her with that weird grin stuck on a corner of his mouth, his eyes shining with anticipation. She immediately knew that something was up. He had followed her to the back door at the end of her shift.

He cleared his throat, seemed to look for his words, which seemed to take forever.

"How's your guy?" He asked Christine.

"Why that question?" Christine replied in an irritated voice. "I guess he is fine. He is your friend, isn't he?"

"The fact that we come from the same country does not make us friends. I met him here like everyone else."

"Oh, well. I did not know that." Christine said as she

was walking away.

"Listen, Christine. I have something important to tell you."

"I am listening," Christine said in a short and dry voice.

"I'm not going to take too much of your time. You look like you're in a hurry. But I just wanted to warn you."

Christine stared at him, starting to get annoyed.

"Warn me about what?" Her eyes expressed impatience and irritation. She needed to go pick up Josh and had better things to do.

"Easy, Christine. I appreciate you very much, and I don't want you to suffer because of him. I just wanted to tell you that the guy's dating a girl from his country. He is not sincere in his relationship with you."

Christine's irritation turned into surprise, then anger... A swarm of contradictory feelings was jostling inside her, and her face turned all red while Abdu was reveling inside to witness the metamorphosis in her. A myriad of questions banged Christine's head, and she opened her mouth to talk, but words refused to come out. She resolved to turn around and simply shook her head as if she did not want to know more. Yet, she could not help saying:

"And why would I believe you?"

"And why wouldn't you believe me?" Abdu responded calmly. "Do you think I would have bothered to tell you if I wasn't sure? I don't know what he told you about himself, but I'm just telling you to keep an eye on him. I know everyone thinks I'm the bad guy here. I have my flaws and weaknesses, but I don't like hypocrites. And your boyfriend is a hypocrite. I don't know if he had asked to marry you, but if he did so, it's just because he wants to have his green card, then abandon you and marry his real fiancée. I thought it would be good to tell you the truth."

"And why are you telling me that?" She inquired.

"Because I like you, and I don't want to see you suffer. Sometimes people show a face that hides their true nature. And as I said before, everyone thinks I'm the bad one because I show my true self. The difference between him and me is that he is good at hiding his real personality. He is not who you think he is."

"I don't know if I should believe you or not, but now I have to go. We'll talk about it later."

"I have evidence that he is just playing you, and I will send that to you. Just keep it secret between you and me."

Christine turned around and walked away. She was too upset to talk. Abdu remained in the dark aisle, enjoying the moment. Things could not have played out better for him. When he was encouraging Amar to propose, he was hoping he could convince Christine to believe that Amar was just trying to marry her to get a green card. He had been pondering over how to handle the matter and had not expected to be that lucky when he met Khalil through another friend. Khalil was bragging about meeting a beautiful woman named Fatu. He told about the dinner they had together with another couple. Khalil was showing around the pictures when it turned out that the other couple he was talking about was Amar and Aisha. Abdu could not believe his eyes. That was exactly what he needed.

Christine understood that Abdu had some grudge against Amar, which led him to make these revelations that took her by surprise. She was doubtful about the veracity of his words, but she became immediately appalled by certain details that had recently appeared as a red flag. Amar had suddenly slowed down his visits and no longer talked about moving in with her. They had previously agreed that he would move in with her in the near future. But he had pulled back from that plan, and his excuse was that he had forgotten that his contract would end later than he had figured out, and he would have been fined a lot of money if he left before the lease ended. She had also noticed that he had become more distracted and distant, but she dismissed the incidents as the consequences of the recent tension their relationship had gone through. She had thought that he would get over it with time and that he would later realize her wise choice.

And what if Abdu was right! It would be a complete game-changer. Was she going to passively wait until Amar satisfied his desires on her and dump her like an old shirt? Was Amar just another alien predator who wanted to marry her just to become an American citizen and then leave her to marry his homegirl? This was a hypothesis she had never thought about. Luckily, from the beginning, she had already rejected this idea of marriage. Could Amar be one of those manipulative men who had no conscience and who was hiding under the face of an angel? She could not believe it, but with men, you had to expect everything. They can be so petty sometimes.

Talking about the pettiness of men, she could not help thinking about Mark... who had found nothing better than to abandon her after pushing her for an abortion. When he knew she was not going to have an abortion, he accused her of cheating and created an unbearable environment just to find an excuse to walk away. After a long fight one afternoon, he decided that he could not continue like that and simply packed his things and left her on her own, pregnant and destitute.

With her first sweetheart, Jim, she thought she would have lived the life she had dreamed. A life of love and freedom. But the ephemeral world of drug addiction had crushed their dream and annihilated their existence. She was in the worst shape of her life when Jim passed away. Mark had helped her with her drug addiction. It was a miracle she had been able to stop. After he left her, she tried to be as strong as possible, for herself and for her baby. She had hoped Mark would come back into her life, waiting for him in vain, hoping he would admit his mistake and change his mind. And one morning, the news came that Mark died in a car crash. Her whole existence came to a stop. She sank into addiction again because there was no way she could contain all the suffering, the pain, and the despair life had decided to inflict on her. Now her life had become a back-and-forth journey between sobriety and addiction like the endless tide of a rough sea...

Her phone vibrated and she wondered who might be texting her. Her heart raced when she saw that it was from Abdu. Even before she opened the picture, she knew it was bad news. She clicked at it and her heart sank. Amar was sitting at a table with a young woman. They stared at each other with a smile on their faces. Apparently, they were having dinner together and enjoying themselves. She squinted at the picture in disbelief. What she saw looked like two people in love. Abdu was right. She had been fooled by Amar. It occurred to her that he had never brought the issue of introducing her to his friends or his community. That woman might be his official girlfriend or fiancée. She wished it was an old picture and Abdu was trying to trick her. But the troubling fact that she had already seen Amar wear the same shirt in the picture discarded that possibility. The picture was obviously recent.

Now it was all clear, and she was beginning to see why Amar insisted so much about marriage knowing her point of view on that issue. Rage stormed inside her as she frantically manipulated the remote in search of some vague TV show to distract herself from reality. She felt betrayed and abused. She was sick and tired of men having a negative impact on her life. All men are just the same, and Amar was just another man. All the respect and love she had for him was turning into contempt. The only thing she wanted to care for right now was her sick son. She would have kicked Amar out of her life if things only depended on her. But she realized her son was getting more and more attached to Amar and the last thing little Josh needed right now was to add to his pain by her chasing away the only man that made him happy.

Christine sat on her bed, holding her head in her hands. She was on the brink of despair. She was completely overwhelmed by the turn of events that were shaking her life. The two men she cared most about were slowly slipping from her hands. A few inches away, there was a little box, and inside the box were a few pills. A couple of them may temporarily stop her head from bursting with pain and anxiety. But the reality that caused that pain will not go away. It will even worsen when the effects of the pills are gone. She took a look at little Josh, sleeping next to her and her pain intensified. She felt guilty for not realizing sooner that her son was suffering. She

142

noticed that lately, Josh was smiling less. A once joyful and happy kid was sinking more and more into sadness and solitude. The only time she saw his face brighten with happiness was when Amar showed up. The two had become good buddies and seeing them playing around in the apartment brought her so much joy and comfort. Amar was unaware of Josh's serious disease, although he had realized how quickly the boy became short of breath when they did some little wrestling. Amar liked wrestling, and he sometimes liked to show little Josh some technique of traditional wrestling from his country. Their cheering and laughter would make the apartment ooze with joy. But little Josh got tired easily, and they would sit chatting and playing video games. The role would then be reversed, and Josh became the master and Amar the learner. That joy she saw Josh having in the presence of Amar was everything to her, and nobody had the right to take that from her and her kid. Not that mysterious woman. Not even Amar.

She would keep Amar for the sake of her son. And that woman was not going to ruin her life. She was going to confront her and make her understand that Amar was hers. She wanted to comfort herself that everything was going to be all right. That woman would be a bad memory and Josh would recover very soon. But her mind could not rest. The probability of losing them both struck her mind, and she stared at the stark fact: she could lose her son to the disease and her boyfriend to another woman. Reality suddenly became unbearable, and she grabbed the little box...

Amar knocked at the door, and to his surprise, no one opened it. He checked his phone because he had texted

Christine to let her know he was on his way, but she was not answering. He turned the knob and gently opened the door. The first thing he saw was little Josh playing quietly with his toys. When he saw him, he became very excited and ran to him. Amar hugged him and was about to say something when he saw Christine lying on the sofa. Her face was turned downward and was covered by her abundant hair. Amar was surprised that she fell asleep so early. She had to be exhausted... with all the work she was doing at the restaurant and having to take care of her child.

"Wake up, Christine; it is too early to sleep."

He sat close to her and gently touched her hair. She moved a little and tried to turn around, and Amar noticed that she was sweating, and her face was very red with bulging and dilated eyes.

"Christine, are you sick?" Amar yelled as he freaked out.

"You.... son of a b.., did you think... I wouldn't... know." Small drips of sticky saliva were falling off her mouth as she was trying to speak.

"Know what, Christine? What are you talking about?"

"I know... about... everything!"

She was trying to sit up and was visibly struggling to keep straight. Amar was scared by her look and could not figure out what she was talking about. He helped her sit up slowly and pushed off the abundant ruffled hair from her face. She was breathing hard, her face was very pale, and she looked as if she could pass out any moment.

Amar looked at her, horrified. She looked completely drunk or high. He did not know what to do.

"What have you done, Christine? What is going on?"

He was trying to hold her because she could not sit straight.

"You want to... destroy... my... life, but I... will destroy you... first." She could not articulate correctly and was speaking in a slurry voice.

He was totally overwhelmed. Christine looked really bad, and he thought about calling 911, but he was scared. He feared that the police could show up with the paramedics, which would not look good for him, a black male in a drunk white woman's apartment. He could be accused of anything. Moreover, he was undocumented, which was a good reason to put him in jail and deport him back to Africa. His heart cried out for help, but his brain dictated him to stay away. Christine stopped talking. She had a blank look and seemed to forget about him for a moment. He was just hoping she would not die in his arms. That would aggravate everything, but at that point, the only thing he was sure of was that he would not leave her alone. He was staring at her chest and making sure she was at least breathing regularly. He had never faced such a delicate situation before.

"Everything is... fine, my... love. I just need... to get... some... sleep." She murmured under her breath. Her eyes seemed to come back to life for a moment, and she was aware of his presence again.

She tried to say something, but her words were indistinct, and she looked pathetic. Then, she went back to a state of semi-consciousness. Her strange gaze floated in the void, contemplating a universe of colorful illusions. She seemed to engage in an opaque conversation with some invisible creatures perched somewhere in the corner of the living room. Amar followed her gaze, and all he could see was the beige color of the ceiling, and his eyes descended to rest on the horrendous reality that unfolded before his eyes: a young mother struggling in the quicksand of hallucination and a young boy stuck between the wheels of an excruciating reality. Something on the middle table drew his attention, and he could see a small plastic bag with white pills in it. He did not know what it was, but he sensed that was the cause of her terrible state.

He put his hand to his head as if he had been hit with a baseball bat. He had never suspected that the joyful and vivid woman he was watching right now could think of putting herself in such a horrible state. His world was falling apart, and he was in complete shock. He was suddenly invaded by a strong nausea, and he held back from vomiting. He had never felt so bad in his life...

Amar tried to get rid of the image of Christine completely intoxicated and lying on the sofa. It had remained so vivid in his head, and he could not think of anything else. He left very late at night after making sure she was breathing regularly and sleeping. He also had to care for little Josh before leaving and closing the door. He had not been able to sleep the rest of the night. The image of little Josh left to himself in the company of a pitiful mother broke his heart and made him consider his relationship with Christine in a new light. Was he going to pursue his relationship with such a woman? Something told him that Christine was no stranger to the use of dangerous substances. He had heard that once you became an addict, it was hard to get away from it. He had never experienced drugs in his life; he was not even a cigarette smoker. How would he find enough resources to help Christine? It was a fight he was not sure he would ever win, and he did not know what to do. Maybe he should take a step back with this whole thing and first try to convince Christine to get herself together. He knew that without her own motivation to give up, there was nothing he could do.

He went back to visit her the next day and found her sitting on her couch with a pensive look. She looked sober and sad.

"Christine... I think we need to have a serious conversation."

"I know Amar... I very much regret what happened last night."

Christine felt very tense and nervous. She felt embarrassed, but above all, she was trying to hide the anger that was churning inside her. She was angry at him for being the cause of her downfall. She had made the mistake of trusting him, and now she was paying for her naivety. She was not very sure what she was going to do, but If something was really going on between Amar and that woman, she would hold him accountable. She would not let Amar, nor that woman, destroy the fragile structure she had spent so much effort to build around herself.

For that structure not to collapse completely, she had to be strong. Something had suddenly gone terribly wrong, and she was still trying to gauge the extent of the damage. She was going to need all her remaining strength to mend the cracks that had appeared. For the moment, the greatest test was to face Amar without losing her self-control and not let her anger appear. She needed to make sure that her assumptions were right before taking any action. Amar was unaware of what was going on in Christine's head.

"I think you need help, and the sooner, the better. Think about your son. These substances are dangerous, and you could have died. Have you thought about what was going to happen to your son? Apparently, you are the only person he knows." Amar preached.

She imperceptibly flinched at Amar's remark. She never thought about that probability. It would be a disaster if she had to die in such a stupid way.

"You are right, Amar. I feel terrible. I had some anxiety issues, and I had acted irresponsibly... But Amar, I need to ask you a question... Are you cheating on me?" She could not help asking.

He looked at her in surprise. He remembered some of the things she was saying when she was high, and he almost panicked. Did she know something? Was she saying some random words, or was she suspicious of something? Was it a pure coincidence? He was struggling to keep his calm.

"How can you ask that question? Why on Earth do you think I am cheating on you?" He said in a defensive way, asking questions in his attempt to gain more time to think.

"You have not answered my question, Amar. Why wouldn't you just answer?" She said calmly.

"No! I am not cheating on you. I am just surprised you are asking that question." He was almost sweating because he was completely caught off guard. He sensed trouble was coming too fast, even before he made up his mind about what to do with the two women. Did he have to talk about Aisha? And at this point, what could he say? He was confused and felt he was in a middle of a crossroad, not knowing what direction to take.

His nervous reaction convinced her that something was going on, and she felt like showing him the picture sent by Abdu. But she thought about what Abdu told her, and she refrained. She could not afford to lose Abdu's help if she wanted to go to the heart of the issue. Abdu would be the first suspect in Amar's mind if she showed the pictures, and that would create an unnecessary drama. Then she might not get to that woman, and she wanted to handle the situation by herself and in her own way.

"Promise me you will not cheat on me." She said simply.

"I promise, honey." Amar automatically said. "But don't put such wrong ideas in your mind."

"I know, it's just... sometimes it is hard not to think about... I have been through a lot, Amar, and I need to trust you."

"You can trust me. But promise me that you will stop taking stuff that destroys your health. You are stronger than that."

"I promise, honey. I swear I will be fine." She said in a resolute voice

Amar took a deep breath and was almost thankful about the drug incident. It helped him brush away the critical question Christine had brought up. He knew he had a narrow escape, and sooner or later, he would have to face the issue. But in that uncertain moment, he felt closer to Christine. He himself had experienced anxiety and a sense of loss at some period of his life, and without faith and the help of the community he did not know what abyss he would have fallen into. He had lived long enough in this country to know that with stress, loneliness, and despair, it was so easy to fall into the trap of substance abuse because they helped escape reality. He hugged her tightly and realized the complex situation he found himself in. The questions she had asked him kept lingering in his head.

"There is no way she can know about Aisha." He kept thinking, trying to convince himself. But he could not stop the droplets of sweat that were starting to inundate his face.

CHAPTER
THIRTEEN

Because of Aisha, Amar was enjoying community life. She had convinced him to get more involved in the various get-togethers they organized. She had succeeded where Demba had failed. Demba was one of the most active members and would go there several times a week to have meetings, to take kids to religious studies or just drop customers off. It was time for the big annual get-together, and Detroit was the host city. People from the community would come from neighboring states like Indiana, Illinois and Ohio to Detroit and spend the whole day together. Gora and Demba had taken part every year, whereas Amar, who did not feel comfortable in large gatherings, missed the event sometimes. Usually, the only ceremonies he would attend were Eid or Ramadan.

The annual gathering of the 'Magal' was specifically for the Senegalese community. Amar had not attended it for years. The place was located somewhere along the I 96 freeway in Detroit and was bought by the Senegalese community just to host big ceremonies that could not be held at the local mosque, which was a smaller place. It was a vast center comprised of a mosque, a conference room, and classrooms for religious studies, in addition to a large parking lot.

Amar had arrived a little late, and the religious songs called 'Khassides' – poems written by the guide Cheikh Ahmadou Bamba – were being broadcasted through loudspeakers. The saint man was the spiritual guide of the 'Murid' movement, a peaceful movement he created in Senegal during the colonist period to protect his disciples against the invasion of western civilization. The big gathering was meant to commemorate his exile by the colonists from Senegal to Gabon in 1826. Every year in the small town of Touba, located in the center of Senegal, millions of the Murid disciples came from all over Senegal and around the world to celebrate that day. Big meals are prepared by every household of the city to welcome millions of guests. Prayers and praises were sung throughout the street, homes, and mosques to thank God and commemorate the numerous deeds and miracles accomplished by the saint person. The disciples who could not go to the pilgrimage in Senegal organized themselves in the great metropoles around the world to celebrate the day.

Amar was intrigued by the crowd in the conference room, and he sat on one of the chairs reserved for the audience. The different presenters or lecturers were sat in armchairs facing the audience. In the middle of the room, sitting on mats, the singers were performing. Their voices rose in the chilly night, singing vehemently and passionately the poems dedicated to the Prophet Muhammad and written by the spiritual guide. His teachings of hospitality and solidarity were meticulously applied. Any person who joined the party, regardless of their origin or religion, was welcome and given a treat. Meals were served in abundance and joy, and for a day, the good spirits that prevailed in the holy city of Touba were revived. Work, faith, and solidarity were the key principles that the beloved man had taught to his people.

Although he was not specifically a member of the Murid brotherhood, Amar could not help admiring those people, who, through perseverance and hard work, were able to achieve great things such as the building of mosques, hospitals, and schools. They had transcended space and time to raise the flag of their faith on the roof of the world, loudly shouting their love for their revered guide and demonstrating that the spiritual life is more important than the material. For the temporal and the material world, the sky is the limit, but the spiritual goes beyond the sky.

Amar was carried away and lulled by the songs that gradually died down to make way for the speaker who continued his speech. He also liked the way the speeches alternated with the songs to keep the audience awake:

"The Cheikh was and will remain the most revered man in the history of our country. By the strength of his character, his sense of organization, and his spiritual gifts, he was able to build an empire whose foundation was not war and destruction but work and meditation. He was able to give the world a new vision that can only lead to happiness here on earth and in the afterlife. He demonstrated that Africa could implement a model of development harmoniously rooted in the precepts and principles of Islam and in magnificent symbiosis with African culture.

"That man, who had devoted all his life to his Lord and to the prophet Muhammad, never ceased to intrigue the colonizer, because in a world dominated by the race to the material, here was a man who had no money in his pocket, had no weapon in his hands, but by his erudition and his heavenly gifts, had more authority over the population than all the foreign powers combined. His people revered and respected him with all their might. He would have lifted the smallest finger that his disciples would have placed themselves as a human shield to counter the invader, but more than anything, he cared about the peace and happiness of his disciples because he had understood that peace and happiness could never be achieved by shedding blood.

He taught the way to happiness here and in the afterlife, inoculating the love of work and solidarity within the community, the importance of knowledge and faith within the individual. The white man resented him and was jealous of his aura and his sense of organization and had plotted a way to get rid of him..."

Amar listened to the speaker, captivated by his outstanding elegance. He was dressed in a large blue boubou, with golden embroidery that glided in the reflection of light; a white scarf, which matched the color of his hat, was eye-catching and increased the spiritual scope of his speech. In the middle of the speech, one of the singers sitting on the mats stood up unexpectedly:

Once upon a time
In a small village lost in the heart of the Sahel
In a small country called Senegal

A country that courageously fights against the ocean
On the west coast of Africa

There was a man, larger than life
Deeper than the ocean and whose
Mind was wider than the world
I named Cheikh Ahmadu Bamba!

Why Almighty God
Had chosen such a remote place
To reveal such an extraordinary man
Will remain a mystery!
But the work of Cheikh Ahmadu Bamba
Will forever be carved in our hearts and memories.

This is the man who proved to the face of the World
That wisdom and scholarship did not depend on the color
    of the skin
Cheikh Ahmadu Bamba was Black,
But brighter than the stars in the sky.

This is the man who showed the world
That you can win a war without a single weapon
He won the battle for Islam and had never
carried a gun in his pocket

He is the answer to all our questions
And relieves all our doubts and fears
Heals all our pain and sufferings
Incarnates all our dreams and hopes
Represents the promise of paradise and happiness
Washes our sins and deeds
He is our solution for life and death
He is the chosen one and we are the lucky ones
The path of 'Muridism' is the way of truth...

ABIB COULIBALY

After his spiritual ballad, the man sat down, and the speaker continued his lecture. There were different speakers, and each presented an aspect of the life of the holy man, interrupted now and then by songs and poems.

In an adjacent room, buffets of various African foods were waiting to be enjoyed by the guests. Amar felt his stomach growling and thought it was time to go find Aisha. She had already texted him that she was waiting for him in the banquet room. He was peering at a group of women when he felt a soft hand grabbing his. It was Aisha. She led him to the end of the room where there were fewer people and less noise.

"What will you have, my 'lord'? I guess you are as hungry as I am." She said.

"Whatever you choose for me, beautiful lady!"

She was shining with elegance, dressed in one of her loose, multi-colored African costumes, which the women wore with a loincloth and a headscarf. The fabric was stiff and made a small swishing noise accompanied by the tender tinkling of gold bracelets wrapped around a hand carefully varnished with henna. Amar could not help thinking what a beautiful woman she was.

"You are so beautiful, Aisha!"

She smiled at him, and the dimple in her cheek sent a vibrating tenderness into his heart, and he silently thanked Christine for rejecting his marriage proposal. Aisha came back with two plates of well-done beef with millet couscous drizzled with spicy tomato sauces. Amar, who had not eaten the millet couscous for a long time, was delighted. Aisha knew how to make the right choice for him. He took a spoonful of the tasty food and could not help daydreaming about his life with Aisha. She would get up earlier than him, prepare breakfast and wake him up as if they were in Africa. He will have a wife who would take care of him, would listen to his every desire and needs. He couldn't help smiling and looking at Aisha:

"What?" Aisha said, seeing him smiling. "What are you thinking?"

"Nothing... I haven't felt this good for a long time. I am happy to be with you..."

Abdu tried to hide the naughty smile that was crossing his lips when he saw Christine heading towards him. He knew she was going to come back to him. He did not like the way Christine was talking to him last time, and he felt a little revenge on her because he knew that she was going to need him. He felt like ignoring her and pretending he was too busy to talk, but the anticipation and pleasure of giving compromising details about Amar was much stronger.

"Hi, Christine, what is the honor of having you today?"

"I need information about Amar's girlfriend. I want to know everything about their relationship, assuming you are telling the truth."

"How can you doubt my sincerity?" He said, pretending to be offended.

"He has become weird, and he is less frequent at the apartment, so I thought about what you had told me."

"I am glad you're back to your senses? Amar is dating a girl named Aisha. You see that girl I texted you about last time. That's her. I even know where she works at. All I am asking you is not to mention my name in that story. I will give you the information I have, and it's up to you to judge."

"Deal." She said sharply, trying not to engage in talk with him as much as she could.

Abdu was not the type of person to get rid of easily. He always had something in mind. He thought it was his lucky day because, for once, someone was listening to him and taking his words seriously. He wanted to take advantage of the situation because he thought it was the right time to push his luck further with Christine while denigrating Amar.

"Christine." He began. "I've always wondered what you see in Amar. He is not a good guy at all. I think he just wants to use you for some reason. It's something he's already planned. I'm a much better man..."

Christine did not let him finish his sentence. She was already feeling irritated and didn't have time to listen to Abdu's nonsense. But because she needed his help, she strived to control herself.

"Listen, Abdu; I am not here to judge anybody. I am very confused, and I need answers. I wish I could count on your help, but you don't have to."

Christine was getting more and more irritated, and Abdu felt he had to back away. He meekly said:

"Don't worry. I'll give you all the information you want to know."

He was already anticipating Amar's expression when he realized how quickly his little plot had been foiled. He could not help dreaming about Amar's astonishment if he realized that Christine had dumped him. Amar had made the mistake of showing up publicly with Aisha and news traveled quickly...

Amar's behavior had awakened in Christine the old demons of her past. She had grown up witnessing her father cheating and abusing her mother. She had hated her mother for being so weak and defenseless. Her father believed he could do anything and get away with it. She had grown up in that toxic environment, and the first thing she learned to do when she grew up was to develop a hard shell around her to protect herself. She had learned above all that the best way to defend oneself was to attack first. Attack quickly and on time before things take an uncontrollable turn. One day, as a teenager, she had intervened between her fighting parents, and her father had found nothing better than to slap her in the face, making it clear that he would beat her up the same way he was doing with her mother.

She had simply retreated in silence and had come back when her father least expected it. She aimed to stab him in the chest, and only her mother's scream had helped her father dodge the knife, which had, however, hit his arm and left a long bleeding slash through his shirt. Her mother screamed hysterically and jumped to take care of her father, who, while trying to dodge, had slipped and fallen on the floor, wriggling and moaning with pain.

The cold look she had exchanged with her father that day had convinced him that she was not playing a game and that she would not be treated like her mom. She was ready to fight back and inflict a greater pain than she had received. She walked away, leaving her parents in disbelief. Her relationship with her parents went from bad to worse, and she could not wait to be eighteen to have a life of her own. She moved out as soon as she could. While her life with Jim was too blurry to make a judgment about men, because of the combination of youth and drug addiction, her experience with Mark had convinced her that all men were the same. When she met Amar, she was hoping to be wrong. And *this* happened.

For a moment, she thought she might need to pray and go to a church sometimes. There might be somebody or something out there you could turn to if you felt that desperate and dispirited. She had never had a true friend and thought about grabbing her phone and calling her mom. But she had never been close to her, and she could not help her anyway. She could not help cure Josh, and she did not know about Amar. God? Her mom had been a regular churchgoer, and as far as she knew, God had not been of much help to her. She nevertheless forced herself into believing that there should be a superior being above that could, if not lend a hand, at least lend an ear. She closed her eyes and tried to pray, but she could not focus. All she could think of was little Josh looking so pale and sinking slowly into the arms of the vicious illness. All she could think of was that her life was being torn apart by that mysterious woman. That woman who wanted to destroy the little foundation of happiness she happened to build thus far. All of a sudden, she realized what she needed was not prayers; she needed to take action.

CHAPTER
FOURTEEN

Alima hair salon was bustling with braiders and customers. The braiders were noisily busy around the customers' heads. Most customers were sometimes forced to put on headphones to avoid going crazy because, in addition to the pain that the braiding could cause, they had to endure the boisterous conversations in different languages that filled the air with exotic words. The braiders spoke loudly, laughed, gossiped or were on the phone with distant relatives while the TV was on. Carried away by their conversation, they sometimes forgot they were taking care of real people's heads, and it took a customer's reaction or complaint to refocus on their tasks. Sometimes Alima had to remind them to lower their voice so customers could hear the sound on the TV. Most customers would put up with the noise and the discomfort and left satisfied and happy as long as they came out of the salon looking like black actresses or superstars. If not, customers and braiders might end up yelling at one another, and it was

Alima's duty to calm everybody down and find an amenable solution. To prevent troubles, she would go around the chairs to check the quality of the braiding or styling, inquire about the customers' well-being and their levels of satisfaction because she wanted to keep the good reputation of the shop. Negative or positive reviews had a big impact on the choice of potential customers.

People had started to get their tax returns, and for most black women, shopping and doing their hair were on the top of their list. They swarmed the hair salons, and for about a month, the braiders would work continuously for twelve hours a day. Alima took a satisfied look around her: all the chairs were busy, and some customers were still waiting for their turn. Usually, two braiders took care of a customer, but when they got busy, each braider took care of one customer in order to meet the demand. Because they have money at that period of the year, customers usually request expensive hairstyles that require a lot of time. Business was good, and Alima had undertaken some big expenses in Africa. She had bought a plot of land that she was building secretly for her late mother. The house was almost finished, and she was planning to surprise her mom. But her mom would never see the beautiful house she had built for her, and she teared up thinking of how proud and happy her mom would have been if she had been alive to see what her daughter had accomplished for her. Ironically, she was the only girl with five brothers, and her parents had always had more expectations from the boys than her. Now she was the one who was helping everybody else. Her dad had never owned a house, and they had always been moving from place to place. She came to the United States to work and help her family, and now that she could do so, her parents were gone...

As usual, Aisha was silently taking care of her customer. Alima relied on her and Fatima the most because they were always focused. Not surprising that they made more money than the others who were constantly on their phone or gossiping. The braiders would speak English only to address the customers. Most of them came from different regions of Africa and easily spoke two or three languages. Sometimes they started talking in one language and ended their discussions in a different language without even realizing it. The salon represented Africa in its diversities. The DVD player was running an old African movie that was seen a hundred times. All the regular customers knew that movie from start to end. Some customers loved the overflowing energy and crazy atmosphere that gave the place its exotic note.

Ma Aby, the oldest in the salon, could not work with her mouth shut and was constantly trying to start up a new conversation. Otherwise, she would just fall asleep. She also always managed to have a piece of cola nut she would chew loudly. She said that also kept her awake.

"Hey, Kajatu! I told you before, and I have to repeat it to you, you are too naïve." She yelled at a young woman sitting at the other end of the salon. "How can you send every week what you earn to your husband who stayed in Africa? And what did you say again? That with this money he's going to build a home for you to live in when you go back home and the rest of the money, he's going to save it to the bank, so you're going to start some business? Huh? Is this woman out of her mind?" Ma Aby said, with her huge myopic eyes looking for somebody to approve.

"That is what you said, huh? She pursued. Now, listen

to me, my daughter: I'm not a psychic, but I can tell you what's going to happen. When you get home, he is going to grab your hand, and he'll say, 'Come, baby, I'm going to show you the beautiful house I built with the money you sent me'. And you're going to follow him all happy and excited. He will take you to the front of the house, and you're going to dance with joy, and you're going to say, 'O my Seydu Darling, I'm so proud of you'. And Seydu will thrust his chest out, and he will tell you: 'My lovely Kajatu, that's not all, come and meet Astu and Bintu'. And you will say: 'Who are they? Why should I meet them?' And the perfidious man will tell you: 'Well. I married them with the rest of the money you sent me'. And you're going to fall dead on the spot, killed by a heart attack, and life will go on. Take it from an old lady who has lived long enough to know those specimens called men."

Ma Aby was talking in Wolof, and an explosion of laughter shook the room while the customers wondered what was going on.

"Heee, Ma Aby," interjected Kajatu. Don't you wish that on your daughter. You're right; in such a case, I'm going to die because my heart will just give in. But I have no choice. He tried to come and join me several times, but he could not. Time is running out, and we don't even have children together."

"So, get your money together, my daughter. Keep them in a safe place, and when you get home, you do your own project with the hard-earned money. You'll be even more cherished and respected by your husband, and you will not give him the opportunity to harm you. Otherwise, it won't be just two women he's going to ask you to meet but two women and six children."

"How can you be so cruel, Ma Aby? This girl trusts you, and all you do is try to hurt her." Intervened Maimuna, the sworn enemy of Ma Aby. The two never sat down next to each other because they could not stand each other.

"Was I speaking to you? The last time I checked, your name was not Kajatu. Whoever does not want to hear the truth should shut their ears. I just spoke the truth." Ma Aby said furiously.

"I think Maimuna is right this time, Mama Aby. Another woman said. You know how sensitive Kajatu is, and you don't have to talk to her that way."

Indeed, Kajatu was trying to hide the tears that were beginning to flow on her cheeks. What Mama Aby told her was horrible and grotesque, and the very idea of thinking about it made her feel miserable.

"Sorry for upsetting you, my daughter. Ma Aby tried to soothe her. You are too sweet, but life is not. I have seen it all, and if I were half as sensitive and fragile as you, now I would not be here today. Be strong, my daughter and do not have high expectations about men. They are all the same."

And the subjects of conversations could shift from everyday life as they spent more time in the shop than in their homes, waiting and caring for customers so they could pay their bills and send money to their extended families back in the country. Sometimes, on a weekday, customers became rare or nonexistent, and they returned empty-handed, hoping it would be better the next day. Usually, they got very busy on weekends, and they went home exhausted but making good money. The salon was the place where they expressed themselves, shared their joys, and revealed people's small secrets... Fatima and

Aisha were among the quietest and rarely took part in all the sometimes-heated discussions. They often kept their heads down, focusing on their tasks, nodding or making neutral comments that did not put them in trouble with anyone.

It was Aisha's turn to close the shop. So, she stayed late and had to sweep the floor littered with hair, plastic bags, then mop, put away the chairs and make sure everything was ready for the next morning. She glanced around her one last time and felt satisfied with her work. She had already called Demba, who should be there in about half an hour. She still had five to ten minutes, and she decided to take some fresh air outside before Demba got there. She had been inside the shop the whole day, and it would not hurt to enjoy the excitement of early evening commuters heading home to enjoy their families. She did not have a family to join, but she loved being in her apartment and huddling in her bed, watching the news or a good movie on her bed after a well-deserved shower.

She turned off all the lights, got out and locked the salon door. She let out a frightened scream as she turned around. A white woman was standing in front of her and stared at her. It was so unusual to meet a young white woman in that neighborhood, especially at that time of the day. She first thought she was lost or needed some cash, but she did not look like a homeless person.

"How can I help you?" She reacted. Things were getting a little awkward.

They sometimes have a few white customers who wanted to try African braids, but that was rare. Anyway, they were closed, even though some braiding shops offered a twenty-four-hour service during the busy times.

The woman did not answer but was still staring at her. Aisha thought she might have some mental issue and passed around her. She needed to get home and was trying to call Demba when she heard the woman call her name.

"Aicha?" The woman called her name. Surprised, she turned around.

"How do you know my name? What can I do for you?" Maybe it was one of those referrals. Some satisfied customers would just refer their friends to a specific braider, and strangers sometimes came and asked for them. But that lady was not smiling and did not look friendly. Aisha was getting worried.

"Sorry, we are closed. We open tomorrow at nine." She tried to get rid of her.

"I am not here for my hair." The woman said sharply.

Now Aisha felt that something was wrong.

"I don't know you, mam. So, if you are not here for your hair, then I can't help you."

"Yes, you can! By leaving Amar alone."

"Excuse me!" Aisha could not help yelling. Had she just heard right?

"You heard what I said. Leave Amar alone! He is my boyfriend."

"Your boyfriend!" The phone almost dropped from her hand. She held it tight. She was exhausted and wanted to get home, but the ride could wait.

"Yes, my boyfriend. We are together, and everything was perfect until you came out of nowhere."

"Excuse me, mam. I do come from somewhere. And for your record. I knew Amar much longer than you can realize. For the rest, I owe no explanation to you." She said.

Aisha could not let that woman trample on her as if

she was a trash bag left in the street. She would confront her if she had to, but at the same time, she was dumbfounded about what she had just heard. Amar had a girlfriend? And a white girlfriend? He owed her some explanation, and it had better be a good one!

"I don't care how long the two of you knew each other. But let me tell you something. If you think I will sit there and watch you destroy my relationship. You are wrong. And you are wrong big time." The woman was raising her voice at her.

"Are you threatening me?" This time it was Aisha's turn to raise her voice. She came closer to her and looked down at her. She was taller and looked much stronger than Christine. And she would not have it. She looked furious. Christine did not anticipate Aisha's reaction, but she was not afraid, and she knew how to defend herself.

The two women stared at each other, each boiling inside with some indescribable rage fueled by the desire to defend their 'affective' territories. Love is a territory, and women are fearless in defending and protecting it. For a split second, Christine realized the senselessness of her action. Confronting that woman was not a solution. Something crumbled inside her, and the strength and determination that accompanied her slid away through the poorly lit street. Who would ever think she would be there fighting with another woman for a man? But she owed it to Josh. He needed Amar in his life. She wished there was a wall in front of her, instead of that impressive woman, so she could lean on it and cry all her despair.

"I love him. I... need him in my life." She felt like saying. She shook her head and fought back that idea. She did not come to beg. "I don't know who you are. But I want you to leave my man alone." She screamed at Aisha's face.

"Or else?" Aisha said, choking with rage.

"Or you'll face the consequences," Christine coldly replied.

Aisha was ready to trip that strange woman to the ground and beat the hell out of her. The only thing that held her at the last second was she could not afford to be involved in a fight. She had her own worries in trying to avoid immigration officers, and anything that involved the police could lead to an unfortunate outcome. It was not worth getting into trouble, and she slowly turned around and walked away, but her woman intuition told her that it was not over. That woman was desperate and seemed to be ready for anything to keep Amar. She was a white woman, and she had watched enough LMN and Lifetime movies to believe that white women can go as far as kidnapping or killing to keep a man. She suddenly felt threatened and instinctively turned around, but she had disappeared.

She realized she was shaking. Amar had lied to her when he told her he did not have a girlfriend. She felt like calling him at once and confronting him. But she needed to get out of the street first. She did not know how that woman found out about her but what was most worrisome was how she knew where she worked and how she knew her schedule. And who knew what else she knew about her? She could have been armed and might have hurt her. It would just have been classified as another anodyne aggression in this crime-infected area. She realized her life might be in danger, and with a trembling hand, she dialed to see how long Demba would be. She really needed him to come and pick her up. She called half a dozen times and was always sent to voicemail. That had never happened before. Demba always answered his calls, and even if he were busy, he would always call back. That was so weird. Something was wrong. She decided to call another taxi.

CHAPTER
FIFTEEN

Mike was holding his own gun. Finally, he no longer needed to 'borrow' his stepfather's gun. With his hustling, he was able to make some money and was able to fulfill his dream of owning a gun. He had no intention of keeping it as a mere toy. He wanted to use it for real.

Everywhere else in the world, it was hard to get a gun. Well, here in America, it's the land of the free. You could buy a gun anywhere and kill anyone you want. He deserved it. He worked hard for this. Now that he had a gun, he had to prove to himself and to the rest of the gang that he could be a real tough guy even if it meant killing somebody. The idea of killing did not enchant him much because of all the dramas that came with it.

He loathed seeing mothers, sisters and aunts rolling on the floor in the sight of their loved one gunned down and covered with blood. The tears of fathers, uncles, and brothers bothered him. It was all horrible. But he needed to do it. He had been thinking about that guy that once humiliated him. He could start with him. He had been watching him and had waited for that day when he could make him pay.

Today was the day! He took a deep breath and stepped towards the man kneeling before him, begging him to leave him alive. Nope! Today was the poor man's unlucky day. In addition, he only had a hundred dollars with him. He said he had money in his account and wanted them to go to the ATM. But it was far away, and he had no time to waste. You should never trust someone who was going to die anyway. He wanted to be tough, and he had to show his two buddies why he was the leader. And he was ready to do anything to earn respect and to be feared by others.

He could not allow himself to be weak. He heard that killing the first time was always hard and painful. It leads to insomnia and nightmares. Then, when you get used to it, it becomes a routine.

Demba silently prayed as he watched the three teenagers. They hired him and gave him the address of a vacant home. Once he realized they wanted to hijack him, he wanted to drive away, but it was already too late. A gun was already pointed at him. They had him get out of the cab, and they took him to the backyard of the vacant home, where a heap of trash and broken furniture, leafless shrubs and intertwined stems represented the lugubrious décor. The young men had weirdly excited looks, and they seemed to enjoy the sight of his terror. They had barely come out of adolescence, and he had always dreaded meeting that category of young men, uneducated, unemployed, and thoughtless. They often acted out of instinct and never measured the gravity of their actions. Demba was losing his self-control and could not think of what he could do or say to quench their thirst for violence. He did not dare to think of what would happen to him if he failed to keep them away. He noticed with horror that his life was hanging on a very fragile thread that could break at any time. He had already handed them all the money he had, but they did not let him go. They had their faces uncovered, and it was a sinister sign. He felt like he had already met them, but he was not sure. He had met many of those teenagers hanging out in the gas station or in the neighborhood, but he never paid much attention to them.

He told them he would not denounce them, and all he wanted was to be kept alive. He had begged them to go with him to the nearest ATM to withdraw every single cent from his account, but they did not listen to him. The gang leader had violently struck him with the gun, and the blood flowing on his forehead seemed to excite them like some hungry wolves in front of a wounded and weakened prey. The ghastly, inhuman look that the boy with the gun threw at him made Demba shudder. He seemed to be under the influence of something that prevented him from staying still. He would swagger up and down as if he were awaiting some ominous alarm to go off.

The gun was always pointed at him, and Demba was begging the man to spare his life while praying silently to deflect the teenager's evil plan. He wanted to arouse in him a touch of compassion and escape that horrible reality he had never foreseen, even in his most horrible night-mares.

Along with the urgency of the moment and the unthinkable feeling of living his last moments, the film of his life unfolded with the speed of light. He should have stayed in his native Jolof-land, with his wife and children. His plan was to just spend two more years in this country, earn a little more money and return forever to his native village and invest in cattle breeding and farming. He had never imagined it could have been two years too late.

Terror had triggered Demba's asthma, and now words could hardly get out of his mouth. The armed kid looked at the chest that went up and down and felt mysteriously powerful, for he had the power to stop the breathing and put the voice into silence. He had the power to cut off the invisible string that attached that man to life, to freeze the frenetic movement of life into a motionless picture and crush the destiny of a man under the wheel of eternity. All he had to do was a simple motion of his finger. That was the real power. He had so much anticipated that unique moment. His two friends stood a little behind him, and one of them told him in a low voice:

"Come on, man, we don't have all day!"

"Hold on, guys! I want to give this buddy one last chance."

"Are you out of your mind?" The other replied.

"Shut up, man!" he said rudely, throwing a furious glance at his companion.

He turned back to Demba:

"Just give me a reason to spare your life, just one..."

"I have done nothing to you, sir, I beg you, you have taken the money I had. I promise I will not turn you in... I have kids to take care of."

"Don't worry about them. We have all been abandoned by our dads, and we are doing good without them. So that's not a good reason. Give me one last reason because time is running out."

"Spare my life, for God's sake! He sobbed. I haven't seen my mother in twenty years, and she's old and sick..." He panted and was out of breath, short of words and ideas. He felt paralyzed. Suddenly his head was strangely empty, and all that remained was the impending feeling that something bigger, stronger than him was about to happen.

"Ha, ha, ha. That's a good one! An old man thinking about his old mom. I hate my own mom, so I see no reason why I should have any compassion for yours. By the way, do you remember me?"

"No!" Demba yelled. He did not know who that young man was. He could only guess he was one of the numerous young men that littered his neighborhood or the gas station, but he had no idea who he was. And if he remembered him, that meant he was signing his own death sentence. They would never believe him if he said he would not call the police...

Demba's left hand was leaning on his chest, where the bullet had made a huge hole from which the blood was squirting, right next to the heart. He realized he didn't have much time left. His gaze blurred and the mind, urged by the soul that was about to desert him, rushed into time and space in a split second. He saw indistinct figures approaching and shouting his name. These voices were familiar to him because he had spoken to them a thousand times. His wife and children were speaking to him, but he could not hear what they were saying. He could, however, see their eyes shining with tears. All of a sudden, someone made her way between them and ran to him, shouting, "praise the Lord! My son is back. Now I can die peacefully." It seemed to him he was hearing his mum's voice. Now he could clearly see her, looking at him with big pleading eyes. "Is it true, my son, that you are back?"

"Yes, Mum, I'm back!" He tried to say, but no sound came out of his mouth, and he could not meet his mother even though she had reached out to him. And she looked so close to him. His mother had not aged in his eyes, but his wife looked old, and her children had grown too fast. They all came to him, but he felt as if a giant screen was separating them, and although they were running to him, the distance always remained the same. An invisible force seemed to keep them away and annihilated their effort to reach him. Tired of moving in vain, his mother stopped suddenly to recover her breath, unable to realize what was going on. The joy that had illuminated her face suddenly disappeared, and a horrible expression emanated from her eyes. She opened a toothless mouth, and her shrill cry pierced the air and stroke him right through the heart.

"That's not possible! Oh Lord, what have they done to my son?" She shouted and then asked: "Aren't you coming back?"

He couldn't say "Yes." He tried to nod, but she didn't move.

In a last-ditch effort, he managed to raise his right arm and reached out to his mother: "Mom, save me!" Everyone suddenly disappeared from his sight; he tried in vain to remember some useful Quran verses that had been recommended to him in the face of death, but the incorruptible nothingness had already begun to erase the traces of memory.

The hand remained outstretched; and Mike, who did not want to miss anything from the dying man, despite his comrades who hailed him in the distance, said in an overexcited voice:

"Sorry, man, I don't shake hands with the dead."

And he ran to join his friends, content with his sinister joke and proud of his terrible gesture, unaware of and insensitive to the tragedy he had just caused and whose scope, like the cries of a lost siren, were painfully echoed to the other side of the Atlantic.

In a final moment, Demba wanted to believe that it was a nightmare, and he shut his eyes, hoping he would wake up. The pain was unbearable. He struggled to open his eyes like in the middle of the worst nightmare.

His eyes never reopened...

The world was collapsing around Amar. No sooner had he spoken to the police for the usual investigations and went to the hospital for the identification of Demba's body than he got a call from Aisha.

"Amar, I am sorry for what happened to your friend Demba. I know you were very close, and I am really sorry."

"Thank you, Aisha," said Amar. He was still in shock. He already knew that this incident would mark him forever. Demba was like the big brother he had never had, the father he had never had.

"Christine came to our salon this evening." Aisha had hesitated to tell him. She knew it was not the right moment, but it was hard for her to hold it. She was too upset by what had happened.

"Christine? What Christine are you talking about?" Amar screamed on the phone.

"How many Christines do you know? She came to my workplace and told me you are her boyfriend, and you are still together."

"What are you talking about? Christine does not even know you exist. How did she get your address?"

"I have no idea. All I know is that she came exclusively for me. It means someone took her to me. And that's someone who is close to you or me. But that is not even the point, Amar. Why did you lie to me, and what else are you hiding?"

"I did not lie to you, Aisha, and I am not hiding anything from you."

"So, am I the one lying? Did you realize that this crazy woman could have killed me? I told you everything about me, and you deliberately chose not to tell me that you are in a relationship. I should know better, Amar. You let me down once, and I am not even sure who you are now."

Amar could feel the anger in her voice, and he was starting to panic. He could not afford to lose Aisha a second time.

"Calm down; I am going to explain everything. I swear I..."

"Calm down!" She cut him off. "You want me to calm down when you lied to me and put me in such an awkward situation?"

"I feel so sorry, but I swear I was going to have a conversation with you about that lady. I understand your anger, but it is not what you think. I am sure you'll understand. I think I have an idea of what's going on. Aisha, I'm sorry, and I want you to trust me."

"Trust you, Amar! How can I trust you after what just happened? That woman looks desperate, and she could be dangerous. Who knows what she is up to if she comes back? I am not ready to risk my life for somebody who lies to me."

"I am sorry for what happened, Aisha. And I promise to tell you the whole truth about this story. It is just that I am too upset right now. I still can't believe that Demba was murdered in cold blood. If I think that we were still together last night. Aisha, this is too hard..." And his voice was starting to break down. Aisha heard him sob at the end of the line, and she instantly forgot about her own troubles.

"I understand your pain and I'm sorry, Amar. Try to hold on and pray for him. I know it's going to be very hard for you but try to be strong. I wish I could be at your side now, but the way things are going, it is better for me to stay away... All I can tell you is that woman looks dangerous. You must be very careful, Amar..."

And she hung up the phone. She felt sorry for him and really wished she could be by his side to bring him some relief. But for the moment, the appearance of Christine had created doubt and fear in her head, and she had no desire to end up with a bullet in the head. This has been the worst day of her life in this country. Not only had she been betrayed by the only man she had ever loved, but also her favorite cab driver was murdered. The image of Demba driving her quietly to and from work kept floating in her head. No wonder Detroit had been ranked as one of the most dangerous cities in America.

Despite his pain, Aisha's words had triggered in Amar's head an outpouring of thoughts that led to a quick obviousness: only Abdu could be the common link between the two women and him, there was no doubt. How did Abdu know? For the first time in his life, he felt a visceral hatred crawling from deep inside him. Everything led him to believe that Abdu was an unreliable person, but he had never thought he could lower himself to such a level. For a short moment, he felt like calling him and confronting him on the phone, but he dissuaded himself. He was suffering too much, and he was trying hard to keep his composure; otherwise, he would lose his mind.

He could not stop thinking of the dire situation in which he had found himself overnight. There were men who had no right to deviate from the right path for fear of reprisals or for fear of facing the wrath of the Lord. He wondered if he did not belong to that category of people. How else could he explain the series of misfortunes that fell on him in such a short time? He had lost Demba, and he was about to lose Aisha and maybe even his life. He did not know what to expect from Christine. She must have lost her mind to act like that. As for Abdu, he was so mad at him that he could not even predict how he would react when they met.

Now that he was pushed to the wall, he had to make his decision. His choice was already on Aisha because she was ready for a serious and long-term relationship, and he was certain that she would make him happy. With Christine, he felt it would be the opposite, it would be up to him to fight to make her happy, and he had lost confidence in their relationship and was not sure he would succeed. He felt that he was climbing a mountain with Christine and that, under the spell of passion, the climbing seemed easy and pleasant, but once they got to the top, the descent could be brutal, and they were getting to that stage already, earlier than expected. With Aisha, life would be a walk along a savannah, with thunderstorms and foggy days, but they would reach their destination together. It was easier to receive happiness than to give it. And now he was convinced that Aisha would be offering it and Christine would be demanding it.

CHAPTER
SIXTEEN

The community had gathered at the Mosque at Five Mile Road. A silent crowd broken by the senseless and heinous crime, committed apparently by lost and disoriented kids, who had killed without remorse or regret, out of ignorance for having never learned to appreciate the true meaning of life. The same question came up in everyone's mind. What for? And nobody could find a plausible answer. And why him? Simply because he was in the wrong place at the wrong moment. Which again comes down to the same point that he died in vain.

More than in any country in the world, it was this constant, invisible, and unexplained threat that made the United States special. It was the land of great freedom but also the land of sudden death where murder could be perpetrated at any moment in the name of the same freedom that allows anyone to carry guns. And death could even come from those who were supposed to protect the population, the police, especially if one has black skin and does not have enough self-control under certain circumstances. But more than anything else, black people are the most imminent threat to themselves. Demba was not killed by the police. He was not killed by a white man. He was killed by another black man, one that called him 'bro' in the street.

The corpse wrapped in a black blanket was placed before the audience, who meditated desperately about the senseless and cruel fate of the man lying before them. Punishment, brutal death was supposed to be the fate of non-believers, hypocrites, and bad guys. And the man that was laying on the ground was none of that. He had all the required qualities to finish his earthly life well. He did not deserve at all that kind of cruel death. He had worked all his life to support his family, who had remained in the country, and he had always been a role model in the community. The equation of good and evil was harder and more complex than math or sciences. How could such a good and positive person fall into the hands of the devil? What protecting angel had failed his job and let that happen?

The cleric, dressed in a long dark boubou, advanced solemnly and started to address the crowd before the mortuary prayer:

"This man, lying down in front of us, and whose name was Demba, was a good and distinguished member of our community. His availability, his love for his neighbor, his goodness and his modesty were limitless. Today we have lost a brother, a friend, a confident, and a tireless worker who has never ceased to serve us, who has never ceased to serve our wives, sisters, and children.

"A hero has fallen after having struggled thirty years

of his life to feed his family. He was planning to go back to Africa. He has never been given a chance to say goodbye to them, to shake their hand one last time. His mother, his wives, his children all had hoped to see him again and to welcome him as a hero after so many years spent on the other side of the world, fighting to give them a comfortable life. He had hoped to return soon to be with his family.

"Unfortunately, fate had decided otherwise. It was written that he was going to meet some heartless creatures that put an end to his life for no reason. People that do not know the meaning of life, and sow death without taking a moment to reflect on their actions. To live is to love, to live is to have a purpose, to live is to make people happy so you can benefit from that happiness, and all of those have one thing in common: the heart.

"A hollow heart devoid of love and compassion has only one purpose: do harm to other people. The person with a hollow heart is a dead man, a modern zombie who lives among us and whose only difference with the old zombies is the way they take your life. But they have the same goals: expand the community of the dead.

"It is our duty and the duty of the whole community to revive these dead hearts because what happened to Demba can happen to all of us. The work that awaits us as Muslims, Christians, Jews, Protestants, or any person concerned with fighting this scourge, is enormous. Our streets are filled with those hollow hearts, and almost all of them are still babies because the world is moving the wrong way. Most of these young people have no spiritual or moral foundation, and they simply think that killing for twenty dollars is acceptable because their sick minds never signal them that a billion dollars would not bring back a life... lost because of twenty dollars. And the worst part is that they don't care. They don't know the meaning of repentance.

"In this beautiful country that shelters us, why so much ugliness and hatred, why so much meanness and wickedness, so many losses of unnecessary lives? Those who committed this crime do not know the extent of the disaster they have caused. They not only murdered a man, but they also killed the hope of an old mother who, after so many years of waiting, had just one last wish: to see her son alive. They killed the hope of women and children who, after so many years of expectations, hoped to finally reunite with their dear father and husband. They killed a clan, a community that relied on the sweat of this man to feed and take care of them, a man who was as valiant as a soldier.

"In a world where it is easier to judge and condemn, may God give us the strength to love and forgive. In a world where atrocity has become commonplace, may God nourish in our hearts the love of peace and compassion. In a world where taking life is easier than offering a gift, may God reveal to us the importance of the most precious gift that no one can replace. May God keep us away from hatred and resentment. May God make that the gaze we exchange with others sends back to us the image of ourselves and not the image of indifference and rejection."

"Amen. Amen," whispered the audience. The religious guide asked the crowd to stand tightly behind him and began praying in a low voice for the deceased...

After the prayer, the Imam addressed the crowd one last time:

"Dear brothers and sisters, as you already know, one

of the last wishes of the deceased, as for any of us, is to go and rest in his country of origin. God only knows what fate holds for all of us, but that is our wish too. You have proven your strength of mobilization in the past, you have shown it now, and I am sure that together we will always face the challenges of difficult times. This present moment is one of the most painful but also one of the most reassuring because each of us present will be able to look each other in the eye and think that the day when we die, we will not be by ourselves. The entire community will be with us. The leaders of our association have already released a certain amount in the solidarity fund, and your support more than ever is needed to face the costs of repatriation. We intend to repatriate the body as soon as possible, and the process is already underway at the consulate level. And while we are aware that life and death go hand in hand, we pray that God will save us from these kinds of encounters as much as possible. May peace be with you!"

Amar looked at the coffin of his friend, the image of a lively and active man who suddenly became an inert and lifeless thing, and he could not help but wonder about the meaning of life or destiny. He had received so much practical advice from this man, so much benevolence and comfort. He felt an urgent need to go and hold on to the coffin and never let go. He could not believe Demba just did this to him: leave him when he needed him the most. He had gone through all sorts of hardships in life, but this was more than he could bear. He felt his legs failing progressively. He tried to resist and keep his posture, but his strength was letting him down, and he slumped heavily to the ground. Painful sobs he had tried to stifle churned through his throat. He felt vanquished, and he let off the pain of an entire existence battered by fate. Gora pulled him out of the crowd...

Back to the apartment, Amar rushed into his room and threw himself on the bed. He pulled his blanket over him and curled up. He wanted to make himself as small as possible and stop thinking. What was happening to him was too much for his brain, and he wished he had the ability of these animals who went into hibernation and slept for a whole season. He wanted to sleep a whole year and wake up with amnesia, or better, wake up and realize that he had just had a long nightmare. He hoped that Demba would knock at his door in the morning again like he did in the past to remind him of the morning prayers. But the pain in his heart reminded him that reality was much more tenacious than a simple wish and prevented him from unloading his sadness and sorrow into the trash can of oblivion. He had to empty his heart, or his brain would burst or go insane. Tears erupted again, this time in silence, without him trying to restrain them, letting himself go adrift the river of boundless pain. After a moment, he was exhausted and plunged into a deep sleep.

Walking fast, breathless, and sweaty, the small group of kids was moving happily through the winding paths that led to the mango fields. It was in the middle of Ramadan, and everyone looked starved and tired, but the reward that awaited at the end of the journey aroused joy and cheerfulness. All of them had left their homes, pretending they had fasted. They had woken up in the early morning to eat and drink with the adults, promising that they would abstain from eating until sunset. But they had kept a secret smile in their innocent tiny heads, knowing they would break the fasting at the first opportunity. As convened, they were going to meet in one of these places unsuspected by the parents. It was the summer vacation, and it was easy to escape the vigilance of the adults. They wandered in the wood in search of unguarded farms. They always pretended to know their destination well so as not to arouse suspicion while scrutinizing the woods for a farm to squat. Most farmers did not live on their farms, and with the month of Ramadan, they usually went home earlier. They were hungry and were mainly looking for mangoes to eat and water to drink from the well. It was the mango season, and ripe yellow mangoes hung heavily on trees, waiting to be picked. They were delicious and sweet, and they cast in the hot summer air sweet aromas that brought water to the mouth.

Amar and his small group wandered for a while and finally spotted the perfect place. They swarmed in the unguarded mango farm, and like starving monkeys, they climbed the trees from which the juicy, ripe mangoes twinkled like yellow stars. They started devouring them greedily to compensate for the hunger and thirst that haunted them all day. But all of a sudden, shaggy heads rose over the bamboo trees that surrounded the farm, and they were quickly encircled by strong and frightening lads. They had machetes and large clubs, and the man who appeared to be their leader had a long black, shiny whip in his hands. They came to them with warrior cries. Amar and his friends, seeing no way to escape, got down on their knees and begged for forgiveness. They were asked to undress, crouch and line up. The man who had the whip started to beat them. Amar was the last in the line and was anticipating in horror the whistling of the whips accompanied by the agonizing screams of his friends. Each whip sent one of them wriggling in pain on the floor like a worm in hot sand. His turn was soon to come.

As in every nightmare, he struggled with all his strength to wake up to escape the ordeal. His eyes opened, and he immediately realized that between the nightmare and the excruciating reality, he would have preferred to suffer the lashes of the whips all day and not wake up. He also realized how much he would have liked to remain a child and never grow up.

He already knew that a bigger challenge was ahead of him: facing Christine. He wanted to call Abdu first and shout his heart out. He abstained at the last minute. What was the point? The damage was already done, and he didn't have much time to pick up the broken pieces. But the most alarming thing was that Christine was displaying a face that was unknown to him. He realized that he did not know Christine at all. First, her drug problems, now her aggressive side. Who knew what else he could find out about her? If she could find Aisha and threaten her, an innocent young woman she had never met before, how would she react with him? Despite his pain, he thought it was an urgency that could not wait. He had to confront Christine, and the sooner, the better. He remembered that he had not heard from Aisha since the day before and decided to call her:

"How are you, Amar?" Aisha's voice was tense. He felt bitterness and a pinch of rejection even though she tried to remain polite.

"I don't really know, Aisha. I'm just trying to be strong, so I don't go crazy with everything going on around me. I wanted to tell you that I am going to meet Christine, and I assure you I am going to talk to her..."

"Enough bad things have already happened!" Aisha said. "I don't know what you are up to, but I can tell you this woman is dangerous. I do not know what is really going on between the two of you, but she seems to be obsessed with you, and you cannot tell what those kinds of things could lead to."

"She has never behaved like this before, and I wonder what really happened. But I can't just disappear as if nothing has ever happened. I'm going to confront her and tell her the truth. I am not a player, Aisha. I wanted to start a serious relationship with her, and I realized that she wasn't ready for that. She wants to stay free and single, and I have nothing against that, but I am a Muslim, and I am looking for a woman with whom I can have a serious relationship. I was at that point in my life when you reappeared. Believe me, Aisha, I had no intention of playing with your feelings, and I was about to clarify everything. I had a conversation with her before, and she is free to make her choice and take responsibility. But I'm not her property. I am also free to live according to my convictions. And in the meantime, I think I have figured out the man who gave her your name and address, but I think the most important thing, now, is to look her in the face and tell her that this situation cannot continue."

He wanted Aisha to believe him. He had told her all the truth, and whatever her decision was, he knew that his relationship with Christine was already doomed, now that he knew what she was capable of. Curiously enough, he had no news about her. For the first time since he started working at the restaurant, he had to call off for two days, with everything going on. And she had not called him. It was one of those intriguing silences that could hide the bad or the worst. But he knew he had to confront her. If he were to conquer Aisha's heart again, he would have to show courage and determination.

He realized he needed to find a new job. He had been in the area for a while, and he knew a couple of places in dire need of dishwashers. He could never work again with Abdu. He was persuaded he was behind this, and something was broken between them that could never be mended again. He should have seen it coming. Abdu had once confessed to him that he was a mean guy, and he wanted to remain mean because 'kindness does not pay off'. He told him that he used to be the kindest person that existed until life changed him and forced him to be mean.

Abdu learned from his other relatives that his wife was overtly cheating on him. He had become a stranger to his wife and kids, who only cared about the money he sent them every couple of weeks. He sent money to his uncle to build him a house, and his uncle married a second wife with that money. People in his own family kept lying to him about getting sick and needing money for hospital bills. Even his own mom only called him when she needed money. With time and distance, he lost faith in his family. The bitterness of his life poured into his heart, and he did not want to see anybody happy around him.

Amar knew he, too, could have been mean because life had never been tender to him. His late uncle had always been a weak person, and his two aunties had been very abusive in his childhood. They made him do chores after chores and never fed him enough. He was beaten and neglected. But now that he was in the US and they were old and poor, they often called him for money. If he had tried to remember all the bad things they did to him, he would never have sent any money. But he always tried to help them as much as he could. You always have choices in life, and between the good and the bad, he would always choose to do good if he could.

CHAPTER
SEVENTEEN

Amar knocked on Christine's door. She opened and silently stared at him for a moment. She let him in, and the look on her face was clueless. Amar hesitated for a moment, said a silent prayer, wondering if it was not a mistake to enter the apartment after what happened. He realized he should have called to meet her in a public place so they could talk safely. He felt a sudden urge to back out, but the door was already locked, and he bravely headed to the living room.

"Where is my little friend?" He tried to break the ice, but there was no answer. Little Josh must be sleeping. He would have run to him as soon as he heard his voice.

The apartment was eerily silent, and half of the living room lights were off, deepening the uneasy feeling that was crawling inside Amar.

He sat on the couch, and Christine sat wearily, facing him. Something in her look told him she was a little drunk or high, but he could clearly see the contempt in her face:

"Is there anything I should know, Amar?" She said in a plain voice.

Amar didn't know where to start, but he had come to tell the truth. He had considered doing it earlier, but events had rushed ahead of him, putting him in a situation that he had not anticipated. He should have had that conversation a couple of weeks before and could have prevented some unnecessary drama between Aisha and Christine. He tried to redeem himself by thinking that he truly sought to build a genuine relationship with Christine, but he had not counted on the fate that had thrown him into Aisha's path again. If Christine had accepted his proposal, perhaps they would not get to that point because he was a loyal and honest man.

What scared him now was Christine's unpredictable reaction. He never thought she could be so bold, and that had changed everything. He had to make a choice, and he had to make it fast before it was too late. He prayed silently to chase away the anxiety that was invading him.

"I am aware of what happened at the hair salon. Aisha told me about it." He said hesitantly.

"Oh, Aisha! And who is Aisha? And what happened?" Christine said with a bitter sarcasm while her voice tried to conceal her wrath.

"I was going to tell you about her, Christine. She is a woman I have known in the past and who..."

"I don't need to know anything about her." She exploded, stopping him. "So that was your plan? To marry me for some obscure reason, then sneak out with your lifelong girlfriend. Amar, do I look like an idiot?" The brightness in her eyes was unbearable.

"I swear to God, that it is not what you think," Amar

said in a guilty voice.

"I could not believe it when Abdu told me you wanted to marry me only because you needed to have your green card. Was it all I meant to you? A way to reach your goal?" She asked him with a contained anger.

"Listen to me, Christine. I don't know what makes you believe that." Her mentioning Abdu's name revived a fury in him that swept away his guilty feelings. He found his normal voice again, and he wanted to make things clear. "But I swear it is not what you think. It's time to clarify our disagreements and find a solution. You already knew my position on our relationship. Things were not really moving forward. I love you, and I didn't just want a part of you. I wanted all of you, and it was difficult for me to go on like that. I'm sorry, Christine... but you are not entirely blameless in this situation."

"If you are truly sincere in your intentions, you do not have to insist on marriage. I am against the principle, but... Who knows?... If you really show me that you are sincere, I wouldn't mind doing it one day. But you will have to forget about that woman and chase the doubt out of my head." Christine said in a subdued voice. She apparently did not want to fight.

Amar did not know how to react. He suddenly felt guilty and embarrassed. He came with the firm decision to let Christine know he had made his choice on Aisha. He just realized it was not that simple. Christine did not deserve what he was about to say, but he had to. He took a deep breath and decided to take the plunge.

"I don't know what Abdu told you about me, but he did not tell you the truth. I realized lately the kind of person he is. But to come back to our relationship, I made up my mind Christine. We can no longer move forward with it, and all I am asking from you is to leave that woman alone. She has nothing to do with this." He said, trying to keep his voice neutral and make the words the least hurtful as possible.

He could feel the pain gnawing into Christine's heart and felt sorry for a moment, but he was convinced he did the right thing. The truth could be devastating sometimes. He couldn't just do otherwise.

"You mean you are breaking up with me?" She said after a pause, trying to figure out what his words meant. His guilty silence annoyed Christine, and she started screaming: "Have you lost your voice suddenly? Tell me, huh? That's what you are here for? Coming to my apartment and telling me to my face that you are breaking up with me?"

She sprang up, and before he knew it, a heavy slap landed on his cheek. For a second, surprise and pain paralyzed him, and he got up, facing her. They stared at each other. He was voiceless and stunned. He did not expect things to escalate so fast.

"So everything was true, huh? I tried to convince myself that maybe Abdu was wrong, maybe that woman was just a friend. I fooled myself into believing you were the best thing that happened to me." She let out a mirthless laugh, looking around as if she was talking to some invisible witnesses.

She approached him and grabbed him by the collar: "You shamelessly lied to me. I asked you if you were cheating on me, Amar, and you said no to my face. Why? Why?" She was shaking him vigorously to get an answer.

He just stood there, speechless, hypnotized by the

pain reflecting through her eyes. Big tears started to pearl on her face, and he felt ashamed of himself. He felt like holding her in his hands and comforting her. He knew he had no right to do so: it would just hurt more. She left him and shuffled wearily to the couch, where she sank, holding her head. He wished he could say something. No words could dissipate the pain that filled the apartment. He felt like sneaking out without a word, but that would be too cowardly. She did not deserve that. Little Josh did not deserve that either. He suddenly felt weak and needed to sit for a while. But he had turned himself into a stranger, and there was no room for him anymore. He lowered his head and proceeded to the door.

"And what about Josh?" Her voice rang behind him. She was almost reading his thoughts. "The poor little thing loved you Amar... and he is... very sick... You have no right." She sobbed. He instinctively rushed to her:

"What's wrong with Josh?" He grabbed her hand without realizing it.

She abruptly pulled her hand back, yelling. "Don't ever touch me again!" He stepped back quickly, but he could not help asking her again.

"What's wrong with him?"

"Why do you even care?" What he was seeing in her eyes now was hatred, and he wondered how quickly love could turn into hatred in just a matter of seconds. An uneasy silence followed. Then Christine poured her heart out. It was a mixture of anger, supplication and sarcasm.

"I opened my heart and my life to you, Amar. I was ready to do anything for you. You said you wanted to marry me? Yes, let's do it now or tomorrow. I will be your wife, and you will be my husband, and we'll be happy forever. You'll be mine, and I'll be yours. Isn't it beautiful? And your God will be happy about you because you are the best man that can be, sinless and pure. Are you happy now? Are you going to stop seeing that woman now? You have to be truthful to your wife, and I am your wife. I will be a good wife, submissive and caring, and I will stop doing drugs and take care of my husband and kids. And we'll have a lot of them, every two or three years, right? Is that what you want, Amar?"

Amar was not expecting that. He listened to her monologue, dumbfounded. Her voice was erratic. She was frantically gesticulating. Her eyes were wild, and she seemed to be possessed by a mixture of excitement, anger, and madness. He was trying to figure out what was really going on in her head and did not know if she was just high or if she was losing her mind. Her reaction convinced him that he was doing the right thing by breaking up with her. There was something utterly abnormal in her behavior, and there was no way he could handle that side of Christine. He was not even sure if she was being serious or sarcastic. He looked at her, and all she inspired in him now was pity. But in his mind, he was already done.

Thinking quickly and sensing she was running out of time, Christine thought she had to use all her options to keep Amar. She came to him and said softly. "Honey, Josh and me, we both love you, and we want you to be part of our lives. He has been diagnosed with cancer. And I know you care about him. We both need you. You can't just leave like that, Amar." She begged him.

Amar threw a doubtful glance at her. Josh can't be sick. He was so lively and happy! He did not believe her, and he would not give in to her emotional blackmail. Christine was talking out of despair, and when women are desperate, they can say or do anything. He loved Josh. But that could not impact his decision.

Christine rubbed her head against his chest and whispered to him:

"What do you want more, Amar. I'm yours, and I'm ready to stay with you for the rest of my life. Forget that woman and everything will be fine..."

Amar tried to stay still and calm. He felt like pushing her back, but Aisha's warning came to his mind, and he did not want to make any move that could kindle Christine's crazy side. Her voice had taken on a reconciling tone again, and she was trying to become the Christine he had once known. He had the impression that inside the pretty woman, a demon and an angel were struggling, and while the angel was still trying to take control, he should find a way to get out of here before the demon took over.

"I love you, Amar, and I don't want anyone else to come into our lives." Her voice sounded desperate.

She leaned over to him and stretched out her lips. Amar did not move. He tried to break free as she desperately clung to him.

"Amar, you're not going to leave me, are you?"

Amar sensed that another storm of rage was about to break out, and he wanted to be out of the way before it landed.

"I have to leave now, Christine." He said in a firm voice and tore away from her.

But as he was approaching the door, he heard Christine rushing toward him. She held a knife in her hand, and he would never make it fast enough. Where the knife had been and how fast she grabbed it would always remain a mystery to him. He faced her, and they both stared at each other. He was stunned by the belligerent look on her face.

"I'll kill you first, Amar." She screamed threateningly.

"Please, Christine, we don't have to come to that. Please drop that knife." He begged her. That was one of the worst scenarios he could have thought of. There was no way he could come out unscathed in a physical confrontation with Christine. They were in her apartment, and she could yell for help and accuse him of anything. If he fought her, one of them could get badly hurt, and that also would not look good for him. She looked like a fierce and strong woman, and If he chose to run away, there was no way he could make it to the door without being stabbed in the back.

"I know you have the power to ruin my life. But think in full consciousness of the harm you would have caused me. I never intended to lie to you or hide anything from you. For nothing in the world, I would have betrayed you because I love you, and I am sincere. You're the one who wasn't ready to share your life with me." He could hear his own voice shaking.

"You messed with the wrong woman, Amar. And you'll have to pay." She snarled at him. "You are the one who wants to ruin my life and my kid's life." She stepped towards him and hit him. It was a switch blow, and it slashed part of his shirt. He was able to avoid it, but for how long? The knife looked sharp, and she was not playing. She really wanted to hurt him. They were both breathing heavily.

Amar could not believe that he was going to die and was searching in Christine's eye for a sense of decency. He thought she had completely lost her mind or might be under some influence. He never thought that things could escalate to the point where he feared for his life. The coldness in her eyes stirred a shudder in his whole body, and the image of Demba flashed in his head. He felt he could join his friend at any time.

Suddenly, Josh erupted from the bedroom. He called Amar and ran toward him, unaware of what was going on. As Christine turned toward her son to dissuade him, Amar didn't think twice. He dove into Christine, aiming to strike the knife out of her hands, and they both fell on the floor. She released the knife, which fell and rolled a little further under the small table. Josh was screaming, terrorized. He was confused and lost about the kind of dangerous game the two adults were playing. They both sprang up, and Christine rushed towards the knife. Amar grabbed her from behind by the waist and tossed her to the floor. Christine's head bumped against the table, and she fell heavily, motionless. Amar rushed to check on her. Her head was bleeding, but she was breathing. He rushed outside and could hear the terrified screams of little Josh as he closed the door behind him.

Aisha heard someone knocking on the door of her apartment in the middle of the night. She got up and went to look through the little magnifying glass and saw that it was Amar. She hesitated to open the door, remained pensive for a few seconds, and decided to let him in. Amar's look was haggard, and he looked very upset.

"What happened? Did something happen?"

"No, Aisha. Everything's fine. I apologize for the late

hour, but I called you many times, you didn't answer your phone. I just saw Christine, and you were right about her. She is very dangerous."

"I had already warned you. You met her... and...?" She looked at him inquiringly.

"I don't feel safe in this city anymore. I spoke to Gora, and he has a cousin who can accommodate us for some time while we can see more clearly.

"We! Why we? Now tell me what happened?" Aisha yelled. She was terrified.

"She threatened me with a knife after I wanted to break up with her. We might both be in danger, Aisha, and it is better to leave the city... for a while at least."

"I have nowhere else to go, Amar, and I am certainly not coming with you. Oh, my God..." She said, looking at him accusingly. "It was so wrong of you to get me involved in this."

"I just did what I felt right, Aisha." He tried to defend himself. "Had I known things would turn out this way, I wouldn't have contacted you again. Please, Aisha, it is already hard for me. Don't make it harder, for your own security."

"We should contact the police, Amar. This is not good." Aisha said.

They both remained silent for a moment, pondering over that possibility. But it did not take them long to know that was not a solution. Both were undocumented, and Aisha had already been told to leave the country with her failed asylum case. They looked at each other and sighed in despair.

"You know my feelings and my plans for you. And I don't want to put your life in danger. It is wiser to come with me." He insisted.

"No way, Amar. I had been in five different cities before I moved to Detroit. For once, I had some stability in my life. And now you want to take me to God knows where. You are free to go, Amar; I'm not coming with you."

"I beg you, Aisha, our lives are in danger. We must leave quickly and go to another state. That's the only way." He tried to convince her.

"This is about you and her, Amar! You create your own mess, take responsibility and fix it!" She angrily said.

"You don't get it, Aisha. She's dangerous, and she's capable of harming you. She's obsessed with me, and she might hold you responsible for what happened to her. I care about you, and I don't want anything bad to happen to you."

"And why didn't you think about that before?" She asked.

"I was just confused. Everything happened so quickly. Now I know you are the one for me. I beg you, Aisha."

"You will not change my mind. I'm sorry, but you're asking too much of me, Amar."

"I want to make you my future wife, and together we will catch up all the time lost. I've always loved you, and together we can resume our life where it stopped..." He vigorously held her hands to convince her about the sincerity of his love.

"We can't bring the past back, Amar. Eight long years have passed, and I'm not sure I've found the same man I met eight years ago. I'm not even sure I am still the same person. The only thing I am sure of now is I want you to leave me alone." She said, resisting him and freeing her hands.

Amar felt that he could not be any more persuasive. He had nothing else to offer and sadly witnessed his arguments fall to pieces in front of Aisha. He was speculating about his future with Aisha, but he was not even sure of the amount of support he would have at Gora's cousin's place, nor anything else that prospective city he wanted to move to could offer him. He did not have a lot of savings in his account, and in this country, no one was prepared to welcome a couple for a long time. And even so, Aisha had to agree to marry as soon as possible because it was out of the question that they would live together without being married. Aisha had doubted about his sincerity and his love. He could not even blame her for that. What did he really have to offer her? Nothing but uncertainty, danger, and instability. He was losing, but he didn't want to give up so easily:

"Our destiny was to find each other again. It is true that we both have been through hard times, but God has a plan for us, and we must not let that chance slip out of our hands this time. Everything happens for a reason, and I don't want to lose you a second time, Aisha."

He approached her and tried to grab her hands one last time. She gently pushed him away.

"You have nothing to lose, Amar. You've already forgotten me once, and it's always easier to forget a second time. If your destiny is to leave every time you face hardship, then go. Keep going. I will take care of myself. I'm tired of going around in circles in this country. I found a sister, a mother, a job at Alima's shop, and I'm staying."

Amar stood for a while without saying anything. He had just received another huge blow in the head. After losing Demba, he had just lost Christine and Aisha. Life was waging war on him. And sadly, there is nothing he could do. He turned away and left.

CHAPTER
EIGHTEEN

A slender man was trudging along a dark alley in Germantown in Philadelphia. He had just got off the XL bus and was walking down the street, guided by the delicious smell of Jamaican food a few blocks away. There was a long line of starving people waiting outside the fast-food store. Half of the customers spoke patois, and some were fidgeting at the sound of reggae music. Amar felt very hungry and wanted to order a good oxtail with rice and beans. After a long day of toiling, he made a stop at that restaurant to buy the only meal of the day he could afford. Fortunately, it was quite consistent, and he ate some of it and kept the rest for the next day. He usually started his days with a cup of coffee and his leftover Jamaican food.

His plan to convince Aisha had failed. He had made the hard but necessary choice to leave the city. Detroit was the only city he had known, and he ended up being attached to the Motor City with its straight and parallel roads, its under-populated neighborhoods, its run-down houses, and its historic monuments, a reminder of a once glorious and glamourous place to live.

He had stayed with Gora's cousin for a few days, the time to find a job and a room. He was hired as a car washer, and he could not afford an apartment. He rented a basement not far from his place of work. He was literally living in a hole, and he would come out of it just to get to work. Laying down motionless in his tiny bed, his eyes were staring at the ceiling of the dark room in this populous and rundown neighborhood. He could feel life vibrating above him.

He could not help thinking of how his life would have been different if he had not faced rejection and failure in his own country. He pictured himself and Aisha in their home with their kids. He would have had a decent job that enabled him to take care of his family. But his country had failed him for not giving him enough opportunity, and his society had failed him for not allowing him to be with Aisha. This country had given him the opportunity to reunite with the woman he loved. He felt bad for Christine, and he was not proud of what he did. She needed him, and he literally abandoned her. He could not help feeling a pinch in the heart when he thought about little Josh. He wished things were different. But he realized his feelings for Aisha were too strong. He could not bury the past and being with Aisha was the only way to heal that deep wound that had been dormant inside him all these years. No man should be denied the right to love due to his origin or race. There was no such thing as an inferior race, nor caste or ethnic group, and that was a universal truth.

He wished a lot of things had changed in his country.

They were living in the modern world, and there were lots of ancestral practices that had to be changed or updated to adjust to modern life. People did not have to be judged by their ancestral descent but by the quality of their personality. That rang a bell in his mind, and he realized how much countries and people have in common. At school, one of his favorite quotations was from Martin Luther King Jr, and it said: 'I look to a day when people will not be judged by the color of their skin, but by the content of their character.' And he could say this country had made big progress. In other circumstances, he would never have been able to be with Christine. And when he thought about it, he was the one who screwed up, not Christine. He was the one who cheated on her. But also, Fate had its own way, and there was nothing he could do against it. And it was Fate that had him cross paths with Aisha again.

He hated the leaders in his country for creating such misery that people had to risk their lives crossing the desert or the sea in perilous conditions just to reach a country where they could have a decent life. There would not have been any need for him to travel to the other end of the world only to accept any job just in order to survive. There was so much to be done in his own country, but there were no set priorities for the youth to thrive. He was sick and tired of all those old and senile leaders whose only aim in life was to stay in power; they could not tackle the real challenges with their myopic vision and spend their time attacking the protesting youth. They would kill, imprison, starve their own people, destroy, and dilapidate the natural resources of their country as long as it allowed them to keep the power. That was one of the reasons he could not go back to his country.

The only thing he wished now was that people like him would be allowed to come out of the shadow. He thought of the great happiness he had with the announcement of President Obama's victory and the general enthusiasm that followed. But as Gora had said, there was nothing to be thrilled about with empty speeches, and in the meantime, the authorities were doubling down on immigrants and their families, humiliating them, expelling them, assaulting them. The government has been separating so many families from their loved ones, depriving children, mostly US citizens, of the most basic rights of a father or mother's presence.

He had seen heads of families who had been in the country for more than twenty years, who woke up one morning and were told by ICE that they had to leave the country immediately, leaving their US-born citizens behind. Those kids were agape and awestricken, confused and lost, not being able to understand how they could go home from school and find out their dads or moms were snatched from them... not by death or natural calamities but by some inhumane hypocritical law. Any of those men or women who voted for such cruel laws would end up depressed and would not stop whining if they were separated from their cats or dogs just for a week...

Demba had died, amid the dreams and hope, without any law moving forward in Congress, without any legislation being passed for those brave people to come out of the shadows. Everybody seemed to forget that they were regular hardworking people who only aspired to pursue the same noble dreams pursued by the Founding Fathers. The immigrants and their families were wooed during electoral campaigns only to ensure votes. Once the votes were over, they remained an abstraction, put away in the dungeons until the next election cycle. The political speeches, as usual, were only meant to bait the masses, and once the people let themselves be taken, the promises flew like dead leaves carried away by the wind. He thought of those millions of voices like him, mute and muzzled somewhere in the shadow, who were denied taking part in the parade of humanity towards light and happiness.

The carwash in Ogontz Road was a busy place. The cars followed each other in an endless line. They were to be vacuum cleaned before being taken to the automatic washer. There were three different teams taking care of the cars. Those who vacuumed and cleaned the inside, and the second team who cleaned the wheels and bottoms of the car and finally, the team who polished and dried up the outside after the automatic wash. Amar was part of the first team and had to stand in the cold outside, stooping all day inside the car with a vacuum to make sure everything was neat and flawless. The customers were often demanding, and the Korean owner was fluttering like a butterfly on either side of the shop. One minute he was with the vacuum team, yelling at the nonchalant or the lazy guys, snatching at times the brush from the wheel cleaners to show them how to do it right, and the next minute he was shouting at the driver to be cautious not to derail the cars and damage the rims, before disappearing to the other side to make sure the cars left completely dry and shiny. There was a manager, but the owner did not realize that he was trying to do both the work of the manager and the employees.

The condition of the cars often spoke volumes about

SOMEWHERE IN THE SHADOW

their owners. Some were well maintained and clean. Others were simply in dismal states inside even though the outside was attractive. Amar and his teammates then took care of picking up all the trash that could not be sucked in before moving on to do the vacuuming.

He would spend twelve hours a day in the car wash and would go home with swollen legs and his back hurting so bad. He thought of his job as a dishwasher which was also hard but which he was more used to. He earned a lot more in the car wash because of the tips, but life in the big city was much more expensive.

No job is easy, especially if you don't have a high level of education or don't have the right paperwork to validate your credentials. He had to do the hardest and lowest-paid jobs. He was sadly thinking about everything he had endured at the university to get an associate degree. He had dreamed of being a teacher, and after all these years in the US, his life had been on standby. Like so many others who had not been able to see the end of the tunnel in their native countries, he had been lured by the dream and illusion of emigration. But once you enter this country and the system closes its doors behind you without offering a way of regularization, you find yourself on the dark side of the fence, avoiding exposure and forced to live a life in the shadow, asking yourself if the sun will ever shine again. He could have been a good fit in education, helping transmit knowledge to kids, but he was not given a chance, neither in his native country nor in the US.

Like a dangerous swirl, life had thrown him under the wheels of a merciless fate. He had only one way out: look straight ahead and courageously dodge the stings of the past and present. He wanted to look ahead and not let

211

himself be discouraged or depressed. He wanted to look to the future with serenity until the day when, deep down from the dark clouds, the sunshine of hope prevailed. If only he could have Aisha by his side...

Alima went to the door, picked up the mail and sorted out the bills. The bills were all she was interested in. Most of the time, the rest was only advertising and pre-approval letters of bank loans or credit cards. But as she went through the mail, she saw one that belonged to Aisha. She never used the address of the salon, which surprised her.

"Aisha, it looks like this mail is for you."

Aisha's heart raced in her chest; fear appeared in her face. Did immigration find her location again? She had changed her address so many times for fear of being located since her asylum case had been denied. She had been asked to leave the country, and she could face deportation at any time. Her fear turned into surprise when she read the name of the sender. She took a deep sigh and opened the letter:

With you, no matter what, life promised to be always
   sunny.
Blessed is the summer that brought you to me
Those days that will count for thousands. Forever.

But fate with its dark wing spread despair and
Buried our hopes in the muddy cloud of ignorance
And into the sullen silence sank our world

I will seek for you into the darkness
Hoping you will take my hand and together

We will walk down the sunny street

And over our head the light of our love
Will mingle with the sunshine to make
The world brighter someday...

Those words are parts of the beautiful letter you sent me years ago. I got rid of the letter because I did not expect to meet you again. I tried to forget you, but no matter what, the words had stayed in my head, and they were stuck in my heart. Maybe the day you predicted in the letter had come. We were dreaming of a place where love could triumph over all the backward beliefs and narrow visions. Here we are free to love, and the only obstacle to our happiness is ourselves. Fate had kept the last laugh for us. Let's not waste that chance.

I have been wandering like a lost soul, and from this meaningless existence, you can save me.

I will not return to Detroit for your safety and mine, but I will always leave my door open, hoping that one day you will show up and that together we will take the path of the sunny streets and finally triumph on this dark destiny that wants to keep us apart.

I wish I could face you every night after the hard work and tell you the sweet words I have stored in my heart for you...

You are the spring that could revive from my heart the seeds of hope and happiness.

With you, my past comes alive again. With you, my life comes back to me....

She stopped reading and mechanically put the letter back in her bag.

Christine was staring at the ceiling as she let out a nervous laugh. A little further, little Josh was crying, he felt sick and was having pain, but he was too afraid to ask his mom. As young as he was, he knew that when his mom had that look, it was not a good idea to disturb her. She was high again and was in a state of semi-lethargy in which she perceived reality as through the narrow lock of a door. She had fallen back into the deep abyss from which she had tried to escape most of her adult life. She hated herself for not being able to keep her promise to not let herself be dragged down. She will be failing little Josh. He already lost a parent, and he might lose another if she did not pull herself together. But it was all Amar's fault if she was in such a desperate state. She will make him pay wherever he is. She heard from Abdu that he had fled the city, but the woman was still here.

She wanted to make them both pay. They would pay for everything, even for Josh's worsening condition.

She knew how to get the woman, but it would not be a smart move from her if she acted crazy. She might be arrested by the police, and she would not be able to get to Amar from jail. Thinking about it, if Aisha did not run away, that meant that she might have decided to stay away from Amar. Otherwise, she would have left with him. If she had to go to jail, she had to make sure Amar had paid for all the wrong he had done to her. She would do whatever it takes to find him, and he will regret the day he had met her.

It occurred to her that if she went to jail, there would be nobody to take care of Josh. For the first time, she wished she did not have a child. She was not a good mum, and the innocent little treasure did not deserve her. She unconsciously yelled at him to shut up. She was not in a state to take care of him. She felt a great weariness and wished she could stop thinking. She was too sober, and she needed to get higher. She needed to be in a state where nothing mattered to her anymore. That was what she needed the most right now, and she frantically reached towards the bedside table and grabbed some more pills.

Old memories resurfaced in Aisha's head. Of course, she remembered that letter. She knew every word of it and stored them inside her heart. She was surprised how easily she remembered them, and she realized she had never stopped loving Amar. She had loved him with all her heart and had hoped she would see him again. She had felt hurt and betrayed by her uncle's attitude. After that painful experience, she had never been able to give herself fully in a relationship, and her first marriage had ended up in failure. As a result, she had entrenched herself into her own world and had not been able to trust men. At some point in her life, she had preferred to travel, leaving everything behind. But in doing so, she never suspected she would ever cross paths with Amar again.

For the past few days after Amar had left, she had been seized by fear. After talking to Alima, they agreed that she should stay low in her apartment for a while. They could not predict the reaction of that crazy woman. But fear had found her even in her apartment, in her sleep... She had not been able to get rid of the image of the cold blue-eyed woman pointing a gun at her, and even in one of her nightmares, Christine aimed at her and fired in her head. She had woken up with a loud scream in the middle of the night, and Fatu had to stay in her room so she could go back to sleep. After a week of anxiety, she had decided she could not spend the rest of her life in fear and had bravely decided to go back to work but still flinched at any unexpected noise.

She had told Amar that they could not make up for the past, but she realized that the past could catch up with them. The past had refused to be buried and had resurfaced stronger. She had loathed Amar for resurfacing in her life and exposing her to danger, but reading the letter, it had just revived the part of her that prevented her from flourishing and being truly happy. Was she going to remain passive and continue to live a life without love? It was no coincidence that fate had brought them together after so many years of separation.

She grabbed her phone and searched for the Greyhound schedule to Philadelphia...

ACKNOWLEDGEMENTS

I would like to say thank you:

To the team of Atmosphere Press for their devotion and diligence, especially to Alex Kale for her promptness, Kyle Mc Cord for his vision and perspicacity, Ronaldo Alves for his inspiring design, and Erin Larson-Burnett.

To the Admin and Staff at Star International Academy, especially to my colleagues and members of the Book club, Haley Hofbauer, Leif Batell, Asma Mohammad, Meghan Dyer; and Ali Al-Arithy for his advice.

To Elhadji T. Ndao, Elimane Mbengue and Massene Mboup for their encouragement and support. They are such trailblazers in Education for the Senegalese and African Community.

To the devoted members of Senegalese communities Ahmadou Mbengue in Philadelphia, Fallou Sylla, Momar Samb in Detroit, Papa Diallo in Texas, and Madiama Mbaye in Denver.

To my friends and former colleagues Elhadj Cisse in Milwaukee; Abdoulaye Fall, Connecticut.

To Chef Rocky, Joseph Gardner and all my former coworkers at Rocky's Northville.

To Diamond African Hair Braiding, Maty's Africa Restaurant, Darou Salam Market, Kalahari Restaurant and Yaya African Market in Detroit.

And finally thank you to all my friends and family that encouraged and supported me.

ABOUT
ATMOSPHERE PRESS

Atmosphere Press is an independent, full-service publisher for excellent books in all genres and for all audiences. Learn more about what we do at atmospherepress.com.

We encourage you to check out some of Atmosphere's latest releases, which are available at Amazon.com and via order from your local bookstore:

Twisted Silver Spoons, a novel by Karen M. Wicks

Queen of Crows, a novel by S.L. Wilton

The Summer Festival is Murder, a novel by Jill M. Lyon

The Past We Step Into, stories by Richard Scharine

The Museum of an Extinct Race, a novel by Jonathan Hale Rosen

Swimming with the Angels, a novel by Colin Kersey

Island of Dead Gods, a novel by Verena Mahlow

Twins Daze, a novel by Jerry Petersen

Embargo on Hope, a novel by Justin Doyle

Abaddon Illusion, a novel by Lindsey Bakken

Blackland: A Utopian Novel, by Richard A. Jones

The Embers of Tradition, a novel by Chukwudum Okeke

Saints and Martyrs: A Novel, by Aaron Roe

When I Am Ashes, a novel by Amber Rose

Melancholy Vision: A Revolution Series Novel, by L.C. Hamilton

The Recoleta Stories, by Bryon Esmond Butler

Voodoo Hideaway, a novel by Vance Cariaga

ABOUT
THE AUTHOR

Abib Coulibaly is currently a reading interventionist and ESL teacher at Star International Academy in Dearborn Height, Michigan. He holds an MA in English and American Studies, a Michigan Teaching certification in ESL and French. He has been working several jobs in the Food Industry and Education since he moved to the US a decade ago. He lives in Michigan with his family.

Made in the USA
Monee, IL
12 May 2022

96232675R00135